CW00481764

Nathaniel Redcliffe, 28, was born and raised in the mining town of Doncaster. Son of Alison and Paul. Currently working for the National Health Service. He did not pursue further education after leaving secondary school, so his writing technique was self-taught (that is why there were so many mistakes at first). He had written a few screenplays, one of which received an honourable mention at one 2014 writing festival – and another screenplay entered the semi-finals at another. His first breakthrough was getting a short story published on T.R.O.U Lit Magazine, entitled: *The Lonely Wooden Lighthouse*.

Alex Green

Nathaniel Redcliffe

GREENER GRASS

AUSTIN MACAULEY PUBLISHERS™

LONDON • CAMBRIDGE • NEW YORK • SHARJAH

Copyright © Nathaniel Redcliffe 2022

The right of Nathaniel Redcliffe to be identified as the author of this work has been asserted by the author in accordance with Sections 77 and 78 of the Copyright, Designs and Patents Act 1988.

All rights reserved. No part of this publication may be reproduced, stored in a retrieval system, or transmitted in any form or by any means, electronic, mechanical, photocopying, recording, or otherwise, without the prior permission of the publishers.

Any person who commits any unauthorised act in relation to this publication may be liable to criminal prosecution and civil claims for damages.

This is a work of fiction. Names, characters, businesses, places, events, locales, and incidents are either the products of the author's imagination or used in a fictitious manner. Any resemblance to actual persons, living or dead, or actual events is purely coincidental.

A CIP catalogue record for this title is available from the British Library.

ISBN 9781398435414 (Paperback)
ISBN 9781398435421 (ePub e-book)

www.austinmacauley.com

First Published 2022
Austin Macauley Publishers Ltd®
1 Canada Square
Canary Wharf
London
E14 5AA

First, I would like to thank you, the reader; I really hoped you enjoyed the book.

My friend and professional proof-reader, Ben Hales.

To all my friends and family for their support.

Weirdly, I'd like to thank all the bands and artists for streaming shows during the lockdown (i.e., *The National*, *Radiohead*, *Frank Turner* and more). It kept me (relatively) sane during this period.

Sprotbrough Library, Doncaster

Perhaps my best years are gone. When there was a chance of happiness. But I wouldn't want them back. Not with the fire in me now.

Samuel Beckett, Krapp's Last Tape & Embers

Part 1 – Desby

Chapter 1

No one else is freer than a ten-year-old playing out with their friends during the summer holidays.

"Look, no hands!" Joe Smith yelled, as he recklessly released his grasp of the handlebars.

Daniel Suddlemire turned away from the interview with *Robert Smith,* talking about *The Cure* headlining *Reading Festival* in the latest *NME* to watch his friend Joe flying down the hill of his street on his red bike, arms up in the air, approaching the poorly built wooden ramp.

He watched in fear, knowing Joe's antics would soon get him hurt.

"Don't do it!" his lungs pleaded.

Although Joe heard him, he didn't care—nothing would stop him from feeling the pleasure of soaring into the air. After getting the balance right, the daredevil could feel the adrenaline rushing through his body, as he picked up speed on the descent. The wind blew back his long blonde hair. He grinned as the ramp drew nearer.

Dan's jaw dropped while his hands ran over his grade-zero haircut. His dark brown eyes widened with anticipation, worrying for his friend's life.

The bike hit the ramp then its black tires were free from the plank of wood, the young *Evel Knievel* glided a few inches from the ground, defying gravity, for what was really a couple of seconds, but felt like two heart-stopping minutes to Joe.

Dan's fears came true. Joe crashed into the ground.

"*JOOOOOE.*"

Dan ran over to see his friend, on the floor, laughing.

"You okay?" Dan fretted.

Joe grinned, revealing his missing baby tooth.

"Did you see that? That was so *coooool.* Come on, your turn now."

"No way, I'm not doing that."

"Oh, you gotta do it. Just do it, it's fun," Joe encouraged.

Dan fearfully glanced at the hill. He turned to his friend and shook his head, shyly.

"Please, I promise you will like it, go on."

"No, I don't wanna."

"Don't be a girl."

"I'm not a girl," Dan whinged.

Dan knew his best friend was going to bug him until he succumbed to peer pressure, so he changed the subject. "What's that?" He pointed to the cut on Joe's hairless knee.

Joe pulled up his little blue shorts, to see the damage.

"Wow, do you think that's going to leave a scar?"

"Yeah," Dan enthusiastically agreed.

Joe came up with a brilliant idea: "Let's go to the beach!"

Dan frowned.

"That takes *aaages*."

"It's nearly the end of summer holidays—let's go on an adventure."

Joe jumped back on his feet, eagerly propping up his bike.

"Come on, let's go. Last one there is a rotten egg!"

Dan knew he was going to be the 'rotten egg'. He was always the last to finish.

Joe was much quicker than him—there was no point in denying it. He rolled up his magazine, placed it in his tracksuit trouser pocket, and peddled his blue bike.

Joe raced to the top of the hill.

Dan trailed behind. His chubby legs were getting tired. Sweat showered from his shaven head.

Joe waited patiently for his friend on top of the hill and decided to shout some words of encouragement.

"Hurry up slowcoach!"

The overweight lad was exhausted, puffing and panting all the way to the top. The heat from the morning sun made it even more difficult. Finally, he made it.

"What took you so long?" Joe playfully mocked.

The boys cycled together, side by side. Joe reduced his speed to be with his pal.

The excess fat stuck out from underneath Dan's tight, yellow, sweaty, shirt. Yet, Joe's skinny light green shirt was almost dry.

The boys rode past a group of elderly women, each holding a wheeled bag, waiting at a bus stop, silently. Their journey took them to a poster of the latest Disney film, *Brave.* Next: the thriving wool and meat market. Turning around the corner, Dan almost scraped his arm on the edges of the brick wall.

They wavered through the crowds of pedestrians on the high street. The locals would visit one of eight places in town: *Sam's Independent Book Shop*, *Floweriest*, *HMV*, *Cooplands*, *a Chinese takeaway, a hairdresser's*, *Netto* and *Wetherspoons*. There's always a *Wetherspoons*.

Dan and Joe glanced at the spiteful faces of the men, who were driving to work at the town's steel factory. They stuck two fingers up at their temporarily closed school.

The adventurers reached the edge of town, cycling past the sign saying, "You are now leaving Desby."

On the long open country road, Joe decided to speed up and embrace the openness. No English summer rain, or wind.

Dan dragged behind, although he didn't seem to mind. Dan was liberated from the hordes of people. Here he was free to do whatever he wanted, without feeling the sad eyes of others watching him, or judging him.

"Dan, howl with me."

Joe took a deep breath, then proceeded to howl like a wolf.

"*OH-OOOH*," Dan howled, the least jaunty of the two.

Joe giggled, impressed by his pals' willing co-operation to make such a loud noise in the open. Joe hadn't noticed, but Dan was less rigid, not as uptight, and the only time his head was actually held high was when they both left Desby.

As the podgier chum leisurely rode down the wide and bare road, he gazed at the tall grass on the side. Each strand was swaying merrily under the warm sun. Dan's young mind was away from the world, until...

"Does your mum know we're out 'ere?" Joe enquired.

Dan didn't answer. He didn't want to think about that bitch.

After an hour, the adventurous duo reached the beach. They placed their bikes against some warm black railings.

Joe casually took off his green top and went running around in the sand.

Daniel was too anxious about the people and families that surrounded him. Even at a young age, he was body-conscious, so the shy boy didn't remove any of his clothing.

Joe did three consecutive backflips in the hot, golden sand, impressing his audience. He felt even more smug when he heard someone applaud him.

His chum did not seek attention from others, quite happy to be left alone. Dan could lose himself watching the ripples floating on the calm, bright, blue, sea.

Joe found a sharp shell buried in the grains of sand.

"Hey, Dan. Look at this!"

Dan turned to see his friend, run towards him, his bare feet, pounding against the hard sand.

"What is it?"

"It's like some magic trumpet."

Dan laughed at the notion.

"If we blow it, we can control the sea, bring storms and tidal waves."

Joe imitated a monstrous wave, by raising his hands, shaping his claws up in the air, and scrunching his face to appear more frightening. He roared before jerking his body to simulate a wave destroying a city, making a crushing noise, and explosive shrieks for impact.

"I don't wanna go back—let's leave this town. Go away and never ever come back," Dan demanded.

"We gotta go back, for our mums," Joe proposed a counter-offered. "But how's about this: we make a deal that one day we'll leave together. Like, I go away, I'll take you with me. If you move, then you have to take me."

"Deal."

Dan offered a hand, to seal the deal.

Joe declined his handshake.

"No, we got to make this proper."

Daniel knew he meant 'properly'. He didn't say anything but just looked curious to see what his mate was going to do.

Joe sliced his own left thumb with the edge of the weird seashell.

"No way am I doing that, it's gonna hurt."

"We got to make a pact, Dan."

He moved forward,

"I'll do it for ya."

Dan jumped back.

"It'll be full of diseases and stuff."

"Don't be a baby, now give me your hand."

The timid kid reluctantly gave his soft hand, Dan cringed, and nearly cried, as the flesh on his left thumb was pierced.

"See, not too bad, was it?"

Joe's smile brought some reassurance to Daniel. Two cuts oozed blood from the tears in their skins. The close friends pressed their wounds together.

"Done. If we leave Desby, we have to leave together."

Joe secured the promise with a blood contract.

"Will we stay best friends forever?"

Joe put his arm around Dan.

"We will always be best friends."

The pair watched the sun's reflection on the sea. The cold water brushed against their feet; however, they did not move. The brothers-in-arms listened to the soothing waves, the tranquil sound would linger in their minds for years to come, until being replaced by the screaming.

Chapter 2

Daniel stood in front of a large mirror in his minuscule bedroom. He stared with his brown eyes at the one or two hairs on his pale body, and the spots. Although pleased to have outgrown the body fat, he hated his skinny arms and his frame.

"Why can't I have a six-pack, like Joe?" he wished.

The sixteen-year-old had left the few hairs on his strong jaw-line, thinking his 'beard' would make him look older. Dan also noticed a cowlick on the back corner of his short black hair. He licked his hand to try and push it down, but the strands of hair were resilient and would bounce back to a natural curl. The messy teen eventually submitted defeat and would leave the tuft for show. He should have really woken up earlier to have a shower, but time was a factor. Dan was already running late, so he resorted to using deodorant, excessively, to hide the teenage body odour. On the plus side, it covered the smell of the house's damp, which was shameful to the senses.

"But who cares anyway?"

When the teenager spun around to grab the white shirt from his tiny wooden wardrobe, he stubbed his big toe on the edge of his bed. In agony, he fell on his black duvet cover, grasping his hands around the throbbing hallux.

"What's that noise?" a voice yelled from the other room.

"Nothing, I just stubbed my toe," Dan replied. He didn't need to yell as loud—the walls were thin enough.

"What have I told you about waking me up in the morning?"

"I'm sorry, mum."

"Stupid boy! Get to school now, before I come in there and smack you."

"Okay, I'm going," Dan sighed. He rapidly put on his socks, school trousers, deciding to ditch the blazer and the red tie. The wrath of the teachers was nothing compared to his mum's. Dan knew her temper was brutal enough to not take her threats lightly.

Two streets away, Joe was using his phone to take selfies of his naked tanned body, flexing his muscles and tensing his stomach in front of the mirror. His was full-length, fixed onto a large wardrobe. The bright light in his bedroom not only made the green walls brighter, but his blue eyes were more piercing, and his short blonde hair shinier. It also helped reveal the lines of his six-pack and pectorals he gained from taekwondo. After snapping ten to twenty photos, Joe peered into his chequered pyjama bottoms, to make sure he had enough hair 'down below'. The self-obsessed teen glanced at his phone.

"Shit, I'm gonna be late."

Joe swiftly threw on his school uniform: a white button shirt, black trousers and matching blazer, but had no time to attempt to knot his red tie. Never mind— he'd get Dan to do it for him again.

Sprinting out the bedroom door, Joe tripped on the dangling controller from his latest *Xbox*. Luckily there was enough room in his bedroom to not hit his head on anything breakable. Not his big TV, or expensive gaming chair. Just the frequently hoovered, soft blue carpet.

"Are you okay?" a voice cried out with grave concern, from the other room.

"Yeah, mum, I'm just getting ready to go to school," Joe groaned as he repositioned himself, upright.

"Okay, hun, have a good day. I love you."

"You too."

Dan left his mid-terraced house, quietly locking the door behind him. Joe crept behind his mate, stealthy taking silent strides along the cracked pavement, with his muscular football-playing legs. The moment is right. The ninja strikes. Wrapping his arms around Dan from behind to shake his frail body from side to side.

"Hey, give me all your money!" Joe put on a deeper voice than normal.

Dan laughs at his pal's foolishness.

"Get off me you weirdo."

Joe released the hold over him.

"Can you do my tie for me?"

"One day, you're going to have to learn to do it yourself."

"I know, but it doesn't need to be today," Joe stated confidently.

Dan knotted the tie around Joe's neck.

"Couldn't you ask your mum to do it for you?"

"She's at work."

Joe lied—he was too embarrassed to tell his mum. "Where's your tie?" he asked.

"I forgot it."

"We can just go back in and get it."

"I don't want to wake my mum."

Joe could see the fear written on Dan's face.

"Has that crazy bitch hit you, again? I told you, my mum said it's okay for you to stay at mine."

"I don't want to leave her, she doesn't have anyone else. But I really appreciate the offer. Besides, she doesn't hit me as much as she used to."

Joe decided to change the subject. He could sense that Dan found no joy in talking about his strained relationship with his own mother. "What are you doing this weekend?"

"I'm going to my uncle's farm this weekend—it'll be nice to get away. How about you?"

"I'm taking Gemma to the cinema."

"Gemma?"

Dan appeared confused "I thought you were seeing Claire?"

"No, I'm going out with Gemma now."

Dan chuckled.

"I can't keep up with you and your girlfriends. They seem to change every week."

"What can I say? Girls like me," Joe declared. "Are you seeing anyone?"

"Not really."

Dan put his head down and raised his tense rigid shoulders, in a shy manner.

"You're never going to get your end wet by the time you leave school."

"I feel like I've entered some cheesy teen-flick."

"You have to start talking to some girls."

"They're not going to be interested in me" was his timid response.

"Just ask someone out. What's the worst that can happen? They'll say 'no', that's all."

"I'm just not that interested in anyone."

"You're not gay are you?"

Dan giggled at his friend's ignorance.

"No mate, I'm not gay."

"Cause if you are—it's cool man. I'll still have your back."

"Thanks."

On the way to school, Joe and Daniel walked past an unappealing, overweight woman wearing a stained grey vest. She was sitting on the doorstep of her thin mid-terraced house, pushing a pram with one hand and holding a cigarette in the other. She looked like she was chewing something extremely sour, in-between drags.

The boys walked past the bus stop with a smashed window and saw another overweight pupil, too lazy to walk, her arms folded and not looking as if she cared about anything or anyone.

The film poster that was meant to advise the new *Disney* funded *Star Wars* film, had been covered with yellow spray-painted words declaring; "GAZ SUCKS COCK."

They walked past the vacant stalls at the wool and meat market. On the corner, a man with a dirty green coat and messy black beard used his worn-out woolly hat to ask for change.

They entered the desolate High Street. Walking past the eight places to go: *Sam's Independent Book Shop*, with a sign on the window saying: 'Everything Must Go'. Then *an Indian takeaway, a closed HMV, an empty Cooplands store, a new pizza takeaway, Wetherspoons, a Turkish hairdresser's*, and finally *ASDA*.

The teenagers knew they were going to be late for their form period. So Joe and Dan picked up the pace, as they trekked past the road leading to the closed steel factory.

Chapter 3

Along the dismal grey row of conjoined school tables, a bored Daniel sat at the front, facing the teacher who was giving a tedious lecture on photosynthesis. The two young girls beside Dan appeared to be maintaining their focus on the lesson; however, he was plain bored. The boy's lack of attention drifted towards Joe, who was sitting at the back of the class, uninterested in the topic and distracting himself by gazing out the window.

Joe noticed his friend peering over in his direction, so to amuse his chum, Joe pulled some funny faces.

Daniel laughed at such juvenile antics.

The teacher yelled to grab the attention of his inattentive pupil.

"Mr Suddlemire!"

Leaping out of his skin, Daniel turned around to see Mr Ford's thick-rimmed glasses, pointing directly to the now-apprehensive teen. Daniel watched as the teacher stood over him with a dominating stance, his hands pressed on the waist of his chequered red shirt. Not many people were threatened by the teacher's presence—Mr Fords' green tie was a clip-on, and he had a comb-over. The kids found him laughable. Sadly, Daniel got intimidated quite easily. He knew the teachers knew as well.

"Were you paying attention, Daniel?"

Dan could hear a few of his class members sneer.

"Yes, sir."

"Well, you wouldn't mind me asking you a few questions then?"

Dan nods his head in response, embarrassed to be put on the spot and dreading any ridicule that might follow.

The teacher applied more pressure on the subdued lad.

"If you get the answer wrong, the whole class has to stay behind by ten minutes."

Great, so if I get this wrong, I'm going to get beat up afterwards too, Daniel panicked.

Mr Ford began his quiz; "What are the three main elements in photosynthesis?"

"Sunlight, Carbon dioxide and water."

Too easy.

"Okay, let's make it a little bit harder." The inquisitor paced back and forth to the window, with both hands clasping the highly raised grey trousers around his hips.

"What is chlorophyll?"

Dan answered quickly, without looking at a book.

"A green pigment that traps the sun's light energy."

"Name me two things that a plant cell contains and animal cells do not contain?"

Slightly going off-topic.

"The cell wall and chloroplast."

Mr Ford rapidly fired another question, hoping to catch him out.

"Which part of the cell controls the activities of both cells?"

"The nucleus," Dan responded promptly. He could tell Mr Ford was worried about losing his authority and appearing less intelligent than a student.

"What's eight times seventeen?"

"136," Dan swiftly answered, without glancing at a calculator.

"You're very clever, Mr Suddlemire. If you actually paid attention, then who knows where your future could take you."

"The class doesn't need to stay behind now."

The quiz master admitted defeat and Mr Ford proceeded with his lesson.

Daniel rested easy, thankful for the cross-examination to be over.

Joe was envious of how smart his friend was and had always been.

During the lunch break, most kids were playing outside and socialising. Daniel found comfort in solitude, spending his valuable time reading in the library. He took a moment to divert his attention from *Stephen King's Doctor Sleep* to pry at a couple of 'geeks' enjoying a game of *Warhammer.* Dan thought they were brave, bringing all those expensive figurines to school, where anyone could 'jump them' and take their belongings. Or just beat them for being 'nerds'. Just before he dived into the sequel to *The Shining,* a herd of children ran past the windows. He peeked out the windows; noticing a horde of people running in the same direction, pushing and shoving each other, so eager to see the commotion. Not one for usually getting involved in drama, Dan left the library, cautiously walking towards the sound of incoherent screaming and yelling. He looked for the source of the disruption as he cautiously trod behind a group of children.

"It's coming from the benches," the teenager surmised.

Dan used a blue handrail to balance himself, while he took the steps going up to the school benches. That's where most fights occur. The ruckus was getting louder.

Joe was playing football with his friends on the field. The game was halted when all the players noticed another lad running towards them. It was Sam—Joe could recognise Sam's tall height and long, black, spiked Mohican haircut from a distance. Sam was out of breath from all the running.

"Guys! Guys! You gotta see this, Michael Clark is going to fight Joel Romeo."

Everyone on Joe's five-a-side team was impressed, but Joe appeared more concerned.

"Does he know who Joel's father is?"

Joe and his teammates ran in excitement to see the action. The other shirtless five gathered their tops and joined the pursuit.

Daniel reached the top of the stairs. Two girls appeared from the corner of the dark green IT block. One girl had an arm around the other for support, while her friend's eyes poured tears down her red face. Both appeared to be shaken by this disturbance. Dan noticed the yelling had stopped, though there was a crowd gathering to form a circle. Silence. Dan noticed one rigid pale boy was sitting on top of a bench, his dilated pupils consumed by fright.

Dan shoved his way through the gawking children, to the front of the circle. He stood next to 'a hoody' who had not done anything more courageous than film the whole event on his phone. No one did anything. Not one soul helped. Not one person interfered as Michael Clark laid on the floor, holding a red stain on his white shirt. Holding a knife wound. Screaming in pain.

"I don't want to die."

Daniel spotted Joe on the other side. They stared at each other.

An English teacher pushed her way through the still crowd. Then, right next to Dan, she broke the ghostly silence by screaming. The deafening high-pitched shriek reverberated throughout the school. For Dan and Joe, it would be life-changing.

Chapter 4

The next day, at what would normally be a rowdy assembly was a noiseless gathering. The entire school: children, teachers, assistants and office staff, were all collected in the gym. Among the middle row of pupils, Joe and Daniel sat together on the cheap, red, flimsy, fold-out chairs. All eyes focused on the headmaster, who was pacing the minimal space of the polished floor, with his hands behind his back. A tapping foot echoed throughout the still room. Everyone was waiting for him. Dan wished the boring bastard would hurry up and say something, so he could leave the sweltering overcrowded room. He noticed a man standing by the headmaster. Dan had never seen him before. The stranger was tall, with a beard, wearing a pair of thin round glasses, trousers and a blue shirt carrying a pen in the chest pocket. Dan could see the light reflecting in between the gaps of his thin gelled hair.

Joe's tired eyes were pinned open. To others, it would appear he was gazing at the child's head in front, but he wasn't actually seeing anything, just an empty void. Unable to erase the horror from his mind, Joe hadn't slept. Every time he closed his eyes. All he could see was Michael Clark's tortured face. Those pleading eyes were crying for help. The blood on his school shirt. Joe was brought back into the real world when he heard two younger students giggling amongst themselves. How that made Joe's blood boil. Fists clenched. Resisting the urge to throw back his squeaking chair to scream at them: "SOMEONE'S DEAD! HAVE SOME RESPECT!"

Joe and Daniel turned towards the headmaster. Taking centre stage, he rubbed his bald head and cleared his throat.

"To those who are unaware, Michael Clark died in hospital last night."

Dan heard a wave of gasps. Although it was sad, it came as no surprise. He turned his attention to a girl sobbing on the row behind him.

Why is she crying? She never knew him. Why am I not crying? Why don't I feel as sad as everyone else? Why don't I feel any pain or grief? Do I not feel the way I should feel?

The truth was Dan's not a sociopath. He did feel sad. He'd always felt sad. He just confused sadness with emptiness. Sorrow had been Daniel's longest companion—a black dog that had been biting into his shoulder for so long. It had eaten him up.

The school's administrator took a minute to pause to let his students absorb the trauma.

"The police have taken statements from the key witnesses, but if you have any further information, please tell me or your teachers straight away. Anything you say can be done under strict confidence. Joel Romeo has been apprehended by the police. It's highly likely that he will be found guilty and will be charged with first-degree murder. You will never have to see Joel Romeo again."

Joe was pleased to hear the murderer had been caught. He hoped Joel's life would be made into a nightmarish hell. But it wouldn't. He'd spend his days playing *Xbox*, watching TV and learning a new trade skill like electrical engineering for free. All courteous of the taxpayer.

The head made his way to the left-hand side, facing a group of teenagers.

"There will be a memorial service on the town fields this Sunday and everyone is invited. Until then, I advise no one to disturb Michael's family. They will need time to grieve."

Dan studied the headmaster's guilt-ridden face as he spoke in a sorrowful tone.

"I'm truly sorry; you had to witness this travesty. I shouldn't have let this happen. I've let you down. And I'm sorry."

"It wasn't your fault," Dan believed. Though he never spoke up.

"The school is providing a counselling service for anyone affected by yesterday's events."

Dan watched as the school's head introduced the quiet stranger.

"This is Gareth Hall. Gareth is a professional counsellor and psychologist. His door is always open to anyone who needs it."

"There's no way. I'm going to tell you anything," thought Dan.

Joe looked across the room, scanning the cold stares from some of the other boys. Round there it was a tougher, meaner crowd, not in school uniform, slouching on their seats, with their arms folded. To Joe, they appeared to be unaffected by a murder so close to them. Their blank eyes told Joe that they've seen these horrors before. He wondered if any one of them would easily stab him, or anyone else if they felt like it. It's not paranoia. Joe didn't feel *safe*. The room darkened and a projector screen brightened. The headmaster stood to the side.

"I'm going to explain the dangers of carrying a knife."

Chapter 5

Dan believed *walking helps clear the mind.* Whether it was avoiding going home, or wanting to spend more time together, many school evenings consisted of taking a gentle walk home, the long way round.

Joe and Dan used the metal bridge to walk over the murky, condom-filled stream. They simultaneously leant over the cold rails. Joe spat into the undrinkable water.

Dan gazed at a shopping trolley, with its wheels peeking out of the water's edge. His mind began to ponder. *This bridge feels so out of place. Being brand new. Shiny and bright. Everything else is just so... dull. And grey. How long will it take for someone to come and ruin it? Like they always do.*

The steady stroll had been a quiet affair. Dan thought this was unusual for Joe to be so mute. However, Dan didn't really care. He was in the mood for a silent wander.

Joe turned to his friend and broke the harmony.

"Suppose you're going to write about this?"

Dan shook his head.

"No. It doesn't feel right to."

"Well, I might take up writing short stories."

"Really?"

"Yeah, I'm gonna write a horror film. Not like those newer ones. Summat different. Instead of being a big ole mansion, it's gonna be in a right small flat. With a couple that proper hate each other. The husband don't know what he is doing, 'cause he's thick as shit. The horny wife tries to get the ghost to have a threesome with them. To boost the passion in the bedroom."

Dan chuckled and put his hand over his forehead in disgust or shame of his chum.

"That is gross."

For a minute; the pair started to feel elevated.

"Why did that shit have to happen?"

Joe was referring to the murder. He tensed and curled his grip on the round handrail.

"Has this place got worse?"

Dan was intense.

"I think we've always lived in a shit hole. Maybe we've just ignored it for so long. We've created our own little bubble."

Joe threw a brief confused glance over to his sidekick.

"What I am trying to say is—we can no longer hide from the big bad world. We can no longer avoid reality by reading, playing *Xbox*, going on our log swing on the track, spending the school holidays in our den in the woods, or cycling our way out of this town to get away. What happened to Michael Clark has really burst the bubble."

"You heard Darryl Mann got jumped on the way home?"

Dan didn't know who that person was and was not really interested in the other people's business, yet today, he pushed.

"No, who is he?"

"Mum's friend's sister's brother. He was walking home with a four-pack. A car slammed its brakes to the side of him. Four lads jumped out and jumped him. Hit him, kicked him on the floor. Took his bag. Now, he's in hospital with a permanent brain injury. All for a few tinnies?"

"That's disgusting. That poor guy."

"I also saw on *Facebook*, three Muslims trying to groom this little girl…"

"It's on social media though. We don't know if that is actually true or not," Dan interrupted.

"You're not a paedo, are ya?"

"Of course not. Don't be ludicrous. I'm just saying that we shouldn't believe everything we read. Otherwise, we'd be like most of the idiots who believe the first bit of gossip."

Joe appeared angry. "You can't think you're better than everyone else."

"I never said that," Dan defended.

Joe walked off.

"Where are you going?"

"Shop. Coming?"

It sounded like an invitation, but there was a sharp and hasty tone in Joe's voice. Dan noticed there was some resentment there.

Dan and Joe were approaching the nearest local shop; when they heard a thunderous bang. Three boys and a young girl, roughly eleven years old, ran out of the shop. The young lads in tracksuits were all carrying crisps or snacks of some kind. The clashing sound was Raj accidentally knocking over his stand full of crisps while chasing the petty thieves. Raj stood out on the street raising his fists. "Get back here now!"

Dan felt sorry for the man. He was overweight so he couldn't keep up.

The little girl stropped her arms by her side, yelling from the top of her lungs.

"FUCK OFF YOU PAKI BASTARD!"

"Wait till I see all of your parents."

The fleeing robbers shouted more racial slurs as they escaped.

Their parents won't do anything. They're just as ignorant and racist. That's how the kids learn it because their parents are still kids themselves, Dan assumed.

Raj stumped his legs towards the two friends, his chest hauling, eyes burning red with rage and bawled,

"Have you seen this? Hmm. Have you seen what those bastards did?"

Dan and Joe turned towards each other, not knowing what to say.

Is he expecting us to fix it? Joe wondered.

"I get enough grief from the Nazis. Kids are now coming in and stealing. Where is the respect? Urgh. Tell me. Where is the respect nowadays?"

"There isn't any," Joe agreed.

"Now, I have vandals writing on my shop."

The boys turned their heads to see 'DS6' spray painted in large black letters.

"Is that the DS6 lads marking their territory on the DS5 side?" Dan asked.

"That's gonna stir up some shit," Joe laughed.

Raj added, "This postcode war is getting out of hand. Somebody is going to get hurt. They want to go to my country and see what real terror looks like." He stormed back inside.

"That's nothing compared to Victor Romeo's crew," Joe stated.

Dan was puzzled.

"Joel Romeo's father?"

31

"Yes, it is. They're the real set of hard fuckers. His gang lets the postcode war happen. They let 'em play gangster, as long as they don't go anywhere near Romeo's people."

Dan deemed it to be unbelievable. It's like something you watch in a film. "I've never heard of them before."

"Of course, you haven't. They're more low-key than the idiots who are just wannabes. They don't walk round in massive groups, covering their faces wi' bandanas and hoods. They won't stand out. They'll be smarter than that."

"You might be right, but it sounds too far-fetched. I feel like I've leapt into an episode of *The Wire.*"

Joe has never seen an episode, he's more into *Brooklyn Nine-Nine.* But, pretends to agree by nodding.

"Trust me, dude. You don't wanna mess wi' 'em."

Walking past a boarded window, Dan and Joe came to a familiar garden. Overgrown grass, concrete fence posts lacking panels in between, and a sound of a dog barking. They've forgotten they're walking past *the Hillbillies.* They're not actually called *Hillbillies*, as far as Dan is aware. Although they act like a couple of rednecks. Three imbeciles sitting on a sofa in their front garden, dangling their feet in a child-size swimming pool. No matter how cold it is. Their bodies must have adapted to the frozen temperatures well because they're always in shorts and stained vests.

"Fuck, I forgot about these guys," Dan whispered.

One of them was dragged along the garden by their uncontrollable Rottweiler. Beautiful dogs, but mighty vicious when not taken care of.

"I told you bunch of homos to get off my street," one Hillbilly spat, as he struggled to steady his steed, yanking his skinny, tribal tattooed arms, across the weed-infested garden.

"You two are a bunch of…"

Struggling to come up with anything witty.

"Fucking… gays," he chuckled.

Dan hated the yelling in his face mixed with the provoking dog jumping and barking out of its slobbering mouth. His sensitive heart begins to race. Nonetheless, he kept walking with his head held high and didn't give any eye contact. He steadied his nerves because any emotional response, whether rage or tears, shows weakness.

However, Joe disagreed. Not being able to mask his feelings, he retaliated by screaming back in Hillbilly's worn-out looking face.

"You think you're so hard, bullying two kids. I bet you wouldn't dare pick on someone your own size!"

The hick looked over to his two scowling friends.

"…or have the balls to say anything on your own."

He was quite happy to punch him in the face, though something stopped him. The mutt jumped close to Joe, almost biting his arm. Luckily he flinched back in time.

The redneck now rattled, yawped back, secreting more saliva.

"You fucking dead, you faggot. I see you again. You're dead. Go and fuck your fucking gay mate. You stupid fucking cunt."

Joe caught up to Dan, who had fled three houses down the street. Joe deflected the verbal slander by sticking his middle finger up behind him.

Dan thought his mate was by his side. He felt foolish when he realised Joe wasn't there. During the commotion, his runner's legs unknowingly sped up.

"Screw them guys," said Dan.

"Where were you? I thought you pussied out," said Joe, infuriated.

Dan could detect where his anger was coming from.

"I'm sorry. I thought you were next to me. You know if you got jumped, I would have got beaten up with you."

It has happened before.

Guilt sprouted within Joe. They had been beaten up together in the past. He should have known better than to be passive-aggressive.

"I know you would have. I'm sorry."

"I'll always have your back, Joe."

On the clear high street, Joe and Dan were kicking an empty can back and forth. The rattling sound reverberated across the empty street.

"To me! To me!"

Joe was open.

Dan, who was terrible at football, kicked the can too wide, shooting it down the road.

"What was that?"

Dan just laughed. It was nice, finding something as simple as a can to take their mind off things.

"When do you go to your uncle's?" Joe asked.

"Yeah, I go Friday after school and back Sunday. I think it's snowing up there though."

"I get a feeling you like being away from here. You still promise you're not going to leave this town without me?"

"Of course."

"Why don't you live up there now?"

Dan's sullen face looked towards the ground.

"My mum…" There was a sound of dread in his voice.

"Fuck her, man."

"Someone got to look after her. When the time is right. When we leave school. When she can get some help. Then we'll leave Desby for good."

Joe could see the gloom growing on Dan's face when he talked about his mum. Over time, Joe came to know when to stop talking or change the conversation.

"Are you coming out tonight? I'm meeting Gemma. And she's bringing a mate…"

Dan doesn't normally like to hang out with people other than Joe. However, after seeing Michael Clark being murdered on the school playground he decided to embrace life and to take some more risks.

"Sure. Why not?"

"Great. Meeting at the park at seven."

At the end of the street, the two friends parted ways.

Part 2 – Pumpkin Leaves

Chapter 6

Dan

I turned left as Joe turned right. I am not one for breaking routine or getting out of my *fortress of solitude*. I'm not really the teenager who breaks out at night to meet the girl at the park, but what the heck. You only live once, or 'YOLO'—as some idiots say. This new attitude was brought on by seeing Michael Clark murdered right in front of me. Maybe I should 'seize the moment', or as Joe says, 'don't look so stiff'. I can't help but appear to be defensive. As I walk home from the high street; a large bald man with his hands resting in the chest pockets of his parker glares at me viciously. Naturally, my shoulders rise and I look down.

Eye contact with other people has always been an issue. I despise it. I don't know what it is that makes me so uncomfortable. Maybe, I don't want people to see me. However, this is going to change! I'm meeting a girl tonight, so I'll 'loosen up', smile (not like a serial killer) and gel my hair. I just hope nothing halts this newly embraced attitude. That is why I hope my mum's not in when I get home. Not really in the frame of mind to face her vicious mood swings. One moment she can be so loving, carefree, and even… fun. Other times; she can be nasty, pessimistic, and at times violent. Creeping into my thin, mid-terraced house, hoping not to wake the beast (The Mother). The old heavy door that's prone to slamming, made it more challenging. Still, I succeeded. She's passed out on the green sofa, with a bottle of cheap vodka hanging out of her hands. Her head is face planting the cushion. I delicately move the strands of her thin short dark blonde hair to make sure she hasn't vomited. This time I was lucky. My mother used to be so beautiful, blonde, blue eyes, button nose, and soft cheeks. Now her face looks haggard. With one red shot eye drooping. Her overweight body shakes. I lost weight, not just through running. It was also because of meals being neglected. I shamefully had to scrounge through the cupboards. I'd often find more bottles hiding there.

Since Dad left us, she's replaced nice dresses with jeans and tight, pink, charity shop shirts. These are now too small for her—you can see the flab hanging out of her stomach. I tried to get her help. I've even tried to explain the risks of alcoholism. At first, she didn't listen. Now, it's like she can't process any of the information I'm saying. I tried to leave a few times, and every time I either got hit, a procrastinating excuse, or tears. Of course, no matter the excuse, it's never my mum's fault.

Chapter 7

Joe

I know my homework needs to be done, but I just can't be arsed. I've just spent an hour getting ready for my date with Gemma. Thinking about her already gets my dick hard.

I'll just sit on this comfy sofa, play on the *Xbox*, and just take my mind off it. As I place the controller into my hand, my mum brings me a cup of tea. She's the best.

"Joe, I was just wondering if I could have a word with you?"

"Yeah, sure."

I can hear concern within her soft voice. She sits down beside me. Waves her long blonde hair back. Rests her caring hands on the apron. Her cherry red lipstick smile and loving green eyes say, 'I'M PITYING YOU'.

Hate it when she looks sorry for me.

"Son. Your school called me today. They are very concerned about your grades…"

She wraps her soft hands around mine.

"At this rate, your estimated grades are not going to get you into college or sixth form. Maybe I can help you, or get Dan to tutor you again?"

"Dan has got after-school detention."

"You're home on time and he has after-school detention? Have you two swapped places?"

She giggles.

I didn't want Dan's help so I lied. I know she cares about me, but I don't need mothering. I'm old enough now to take care of myself.

"Please, take a moment to think about it."

"I will."

Another lie.

"I must dash. It's my late shift at the bar tonight. I'll be home at midnight. I expect you to be in bed and not on those computer games."

Don't worry mum, I'll be in bed… with Gemma.

"I love you, Joe."

I shriek when she gives me a sloppy kiss on the forehead.

Errr.

So embarrassing.

Chapter 8

Dan

Sneaking out is exhilarating. The fear of being caught and breaking the rules gave me a mischievous thrill. Secretly, I like the idea of being on the road, being hunted down, never to be found. Living in a tent in the north of Scotland sounds appealing. Waking up to a sunrise, with the light reflecting on top of the calm, blue waters of Loch Lomond. I could wild camp anywhere, not necessarily Scotland. I could be anywhere and be anything. Be someone else, someone who's better than me. Impersonate a more charming, and confident character. Instead of being a shy skinny loser, with fluffy hair, which has one side that likes to stand out. Literally, the only part of me that insists on standing out.

Tonight I can't show any of my insecurities to Gemma's friend. Girls don't like pathetic flops. They like Joe—confident. No matter how much bullshit he spouted, it's still less creepy than saying nothing. Got to stay more assured. I'll raise my head, swing my arms a tad more, as opposed to me stooping to look at the ground, carrying my hands in my pockets. *OK… I'm doing it… it feels unnatural, but I can keep it up*. A gang of youths. They're loud, playing awful grime music. They begin to walk in my direction. My eyes appear shifty. I don't want to give eye contact. My hands retreat into my pockets as my neck bows. That's not the worst part—as they walk past and maintain a safe distance away from me, I'm suddenly out of breath. My lungs are pacing up and down rapidly and my chest is oh so tight. My skinny legs feel wobbly as I try to regain control of my breathing. I was holding my breath. Why did that occur? Was it the group of kids that bounced by? It must be anxiety.

I made it to the park. There's an unsettling atmosphere that's breezing in the cold air. A dying orange street lamp looms over the scorched park slides and the swings, which have their chains wrapped around their supporting pole. Trouble

41

occurs here. Hopefully, we won't be staying long. I don't want anyone else thinking we're being a bunch of dirty scumbags, who like to hang at the park, drinking cider, causing fights, setting fires, etc. Finally, they're here. I hate hanging about on my own too long. I tread fearfully towards Joe and the two girls because there could still be used needles hiding amongst the uncut grass. Joe is wearing his usual baggy jeans and tight blue collared shirt, showing off the muscles in his arms.

Joe grinned, "Dan, this is Gemma."

He points to the petite blonde, with the lip piercing.

Joe moves his intentional smirk, towards a pretty girl with ginger hair, in a white teddy jacket, who looks to be taking an unnecessary amount of selfies.

"Dan, this is Glean."

"Glen?"

"No, Glean," Joe corrected.

What sort of name is Glean?

"Well, aren't you going to say something," Joe pushed.

"Hello. Glean?"

She takes a millisecond of her precious time to come off her phone to reply.

"Oh, hi there."

She immediately goes back to her selfies, returning to her devoted *Instagram* followers. I assume, if she didn't post a good picture, at the correct angle, every two minutes then she'd no longer be cream-of-the-crop and receive numerous angry fan letters.

Time passes slowly at the wretched park. The four of us have been sitting on the wooden bench, a lot longer than I would have liked. I wish we could sit inside somewhere. But where? If I take the girls to mine, my mum would go mad.

Joe's mum would have taken us in—she's a sweetheart. I'm freezing my nipples off, sitting here doing nothing. Longing for a warm jumper, instead of this *Frank Turner* shirt, but I can't be seen to be a wimp. Joe and Gemma have been talking for a long time. Well, Joe's been talking and Gemma is just giggling, playing with her hair. She likes him. She does seem kind. Best not get too close though. Joe will find another replacement next week. However, me and *Glean* haven't exchanged any words. I'm sitting here, wishing I was in bed, and she's glued to her phone texting. Who's she texting? Probably another boy. Someone who's on the same wavelength has her. Someone who is more interesting. I wanted to find something to say. The only thing I can conjure up in my mind is 'hello'. I don't understand how my mind is racing with thoughts 99% of the time, but when it comes to talking to other people, I am unable to summon up anything to say. Most of the time when it calls to be reserved I won't say anything to anyone.

In times like this when I actually want to speak, a fog clouds over my thoughts, leaving my head empty. *She'll start thinking you're a serial killer, Dan. Say something. Anything. First, clear that lump in your throat.*

"Hey, Glean."

She diverts her attention to me, staring at me with her luscious green eyes.

"Do you watch *Doctor Who?*"

There's a pause and a black expression. It only lasted a second, but it felt like hours.

Glean bursts out laughing.

It was a stupid question… of course, she watched Doctor Who.

Joe pulled Glean away from her mesmerising phone. I just wish I had the concentration to listen to their conversation. My short term memory has made me forget what they were all talking about in the first place. All I remember was being uninterested.

That voice returns; *You don't belong here, Dan. You never have done, and you never will.*

I know. I thought this time would be different.

No matter how hard you try to 'fit in', you'll never be a part of a group.

From the outside; I watch three people have fun and enjoy themselves. While I gaze from the side-lines. Alone.

Chapter 9
Joe

Leaving the park, I kissed Gemma goodbye. I do like her. I like how she makes me feel. I really want her. She said she would like to lose her virginity to me. It's a big step for her, I know how important it is for a girl. Not so much for a bloke. But, I'll look after her.

Dan looks up to me, looking miserable as anything.

"I'm heading off home. Are you walking through town with me?"

"Yeah, mate."

He should be able to walk home by himself. Suppose, these are hard times. Still, if he made an effort, and actually be bothered to speak to her, then I would walk Gemma home—and he could've been with Glean. He probably didn't like her cause of her name, it'll be something as silly as that. He's not really in a position to be picky. I've looked after Dan all my life, I ain't stopping now.

Walking up the empty High Street at night, Dan was quiet, so I was still messaging Gem on my phone.

"What's that?" Dan screamed.

Looking up, we both saw a homeless man spread out, on the ground, like a drunk starfish.

Dan leaned over and put his hand on the dirty guy's chest.

"He's breathing."

"What should we do?"

"Leave him."

"We can't leave him here."

"He's probably just on drugs. He's done it to himself."

I was surprised, and not in a good way. I've never heard Dan be so cold before. I couldn't leave this man on the floor here. We had to help. But how? Eventually, the idea came to me—the solution was in my hands.

"I'll call an ambulance."

As I dialled 999, a car slammed the breaks beside us. Three lads stepped out of the car. They're going to fucking attack us! I feel the adrenaline run through my body. The hearts beating against the chest. Yet, I control the pace as blood flows to my muscles. I raise my fists in the air. Pulling my stronger right side back, ready to throw a good clean punch. My eyes are pinned open, focusing on the short guy with a bright red baseball cap, who is bouncing around over the unconscious homeless guy. Using his flashy white trainers to jump over a separate limb. Wooing in a high pitch tone. He's going to hurt him. The bastards are taking advantage of the vulnerable. Well, they can get fucked. A deeper broader voice came from deep within me.

"Stay away from him,"

In the corner of my left eye, I notice two guys, stepping out, one white and one brown, both eyeing me up. Assessing me. Never seen 'em before. The white guy was fat, ugly, with a thick fringe over his forehead, and wore a bright gold chain around his shoddy *Suicide Squad Joker* top. The other guy wore a matching black tracksuit, but not a cheap pair. Far from it—very expensive, *Ralph Lauren* or *Gucci* type. In fact, I recognise him. His name is Leebee. Shit. I feel the sweat coming now. My jaw is going to drop. I need to tell Dan. I turn my head to tell him, telepathically. The little fucker is about to run up the grassy hill behind me.

Was he going to leave me? Again.

I bet he was. His face is so white. Looking so afraid. Coward. Well, I won't back down, I'd rather get stabbed than let Dan get jumped.

Red Hat stopped jumping; "I *tink* he's one of ours."

One of ours? I wanted to ask, but questions could get me killed.

"Hey, we're not looking for trouble. Got no beef *wit* you. We just wanna know—have you seen Nikki Yakes?"

Who?

I turned to see if Dan knew, but he looked confused.

"No."

I paused to clear my throat. Longer than I wanted.

"I don't know her."

Leebee, and the rest of his crew kept staring. They were looking to see if we were lying.

The fat guy in the *Joker* top was stepping closer to me. He moves slowly on the curb, eyes fixed on me. I measure him. Even though he's overweight, there's not much muscle behind it. I guess he's lacking in brains and stamina. A few blows will take him down. He's carrying something; I can't see what his chunky left hand is hiding behind his back.

He's got a fucking knife. I am going to get a knived here on the street. I'm going to bleed out slowly, and die, just like Michael. I need to get safe.

"What's ya name?" Leebee asked.

I ain't answering. And I'm not turning my head away from *lard-arse.*

"*Oi.*"

I looked away this time. Leebee must hate being ignored. His tone was less patient and more demanding. I was going to keep quiet, till Fatty weighed in...

"Speak-up, *motha fucka.*"

"Joe... I'm Joe."

I don't know why I repeated that. My head is racing too much. I start to feel intimidated. And I hate feeling small.

"What's ya age, blud?" Leebee quizzed.

"Sixteen."

Dan moved in a little closer to me. I started to feel a little safer. But he's still behind me. I bet that bitch will use me as a human shield.

Leebee smiled. He seemed to be impressed. Don't know why.

"I like how you'd be protecting ya boy. We look out for each other n'all. We be *fam.* Family look out for each other."

Leebee points to Red Hat.

"Dat over there is Mikey."

Then he points to Bigfoot's Inbred Cousin next to me.

"That dude's DC."

Because of his love for Batman Characters? I assume.

He doesn't say 'hello'. All he offers is a shady glance. I guess manners were not taught in his house. I can't see why I'm the dodgy one? All I want is to go home. There must be something about me he doesn't like.

"You need work?" Leebee offered.

"No, I'm good. Thanks."

"What ya gonna do when ya leave school? Everywhere be shuttin' down here. We pay you good. So ya can buy your girlfriend some*ting* fancy? Take her out to a fancy-arse restaurant. Feel me?"

"More like a boyfriend. His bitch-ass ain't gonna roll wi' us."

"Bitch Ass?" I'm stronger than you. Especially when he still sounds like he has chunks of food still in his throat.

"Ayees, fujokin you man."

No, you wasn't just fucking joking. I can hear it in your hostile voice.

Now the little scrappy dude starts,

"Dis cracker rather be working at *Maccie D's*."

They all laugh loudly. Causing further embarrassment. Because with my expected grades, I won't be going to college soon. I turn to Dan and his face is begging me not to go.

"O'right Joe, if you wanna get some work? Find me on Archers Road."

Leebee gets in the car. The rest of the crew follow. DC waits till last, he spits on the floor right in front of me, as a sign of disrespect. I would love nothing more than to stomp his face on the kerb. I know as soon as I touch him, me and Dan will both be dead.

Chapter 10

Dan

"Every day, more numb to agony." That's a concise lyric by *Manic Street Preachers.* It flows out the headphones at such an appropriate time because I am no longer fazed by the deteriorating horrors around me. When Leebee's car pulled up, I was startled, mainly due to an instinctive will to survive. One trait that's conveyed by our prehistoric ancestors. So I leapt up the hill, to have higher ground.

Oh, dear. Hope Joe never thought I was going to leave him.

I would rather be murdered with my best friend than gain a reputation as a coward. Perhaps, dying protecting him would actually give a sense of purpose to my meaningless life.

A car drives by. I jump. Could it have been Romeo's henchmen coming back? Maybe I jerked because the vehicle broke me from my own world again. Still, I'd rather be there than here. I'd rather be anywhere.

There's a possibility of living with my uncle, but that would leave my mum and Joe. She'd have to look after herself. Any parent should know their offspring will want to gain some independence once they leave school. No matter how torturous they are.

I can't take Joe to my uncle's farm because they haven't even met, and my uncle Clive is pretty territorial. Uncle C won't give his land to any stranger when he dies. Not that he's planning on leaving this Earth yet—I have never seen a seventy-year-old so athletic.

Yet, my thoughts return to Joe. I could live at my uncle's farm on my own. It's that stupid pact we made when we were kids. I know people break promises all time, such as *"I promise to file that report for you."* Or *"I promise I'll get you that money, so you can attend the school's trip to the war museum."* And my favourite: *"I promise to love you forever and ever. Until death does us part."* Until they walk out on you.

It's best not to rely on anybody. We're all alone in this world.

I repress that dark concept. I seal it shut, by knowing Joe has been there for me. That's why I need to keep my silly little promise.

The stench of mould killer and cigarette smoke told me I was home. Without wanting to wake a soul, I secured the door smoothly and paced my steps placidly. Not knowing it was completely unnecessary. I gasped and froze on the spot when I saw my mum swaying into the hallway, with a bottle of vodka in her hand. Her one working spiteful red-eye scrutinised me.

"Where' you been, Dan? Have you been out with those… *girls?*"

Her speech was slurred.

"I just went out with Joe. That's all, mum."

My reply was rapid. She can now sense my lie.

"You're lying to me. I want you to tell me this instant," she shrieked.

She stumbled forward. While losing balance, one of her claws scratched the wallpaper. My heart was beating fast. I felt my throat becoming dry. I eagerly wanted to slide past her and run upstairs. Lock my room behind me. Her face peers up, with growling teeth.

"Why haven't you told me yet?"

The words become stuck in my throat.

"Spit it out!"

She screams in my face, and I shudder in response.

"You've five seconds before I fucking 'it you."

She raises a shaky fist, and I finch with my hands held up.

"I just went out with Joe. I swear."

Another speedy excuse. I quiver underneath her wrath. Whilst expecting another blow to the body… All of a sudden… she hugs me?

"Oh, my beautiful boy."

It's those fucking mood swings.

"I'm just so tired," she cried.

I feel the warm vodka being poured onto my back.

49

"It's okay, mum," I lied.

"I need you to look after me. All the mommas need their little boys to look after them. Do you agree?"

I remain quiet. It's the caregiver's job to safely prepare their children for the world. Within her clutch, she shakes me.

"I said don't you agree," she spat.

"Yeah, sure."

I helped my mum up the stairs. With her arm around my puny shoulders, it feels like I'm carrying dead weight. Exhausted and sweaty, I plunge her body onto the pink, unwashed bed. Intending to retreat into bed myself, after I drop a blanket onto the mother's lap, I turn to leave. A hand seized my wrist, nails almost slicing into the radial artery.

"Son," she wept.

"Yes, mum."

She looked upon me with such a sympathetic expression. Even loosened her grip on my hand, it's almost as if she's holding it again.

"I want you to know"

Here it is, another promise to get better.

"Your dad left because of you."

My heart stopped. The world became still. Rage conjured up from my stomach like bile. I pushed her hand away. Stormed outside. Slammed the door. There I fell onto my knees and cried. It felt like a knife pierced my chest before cutting its way up my oesophagus. I wanted to release the biggest scream onto the stained carpet. It felt as if my jaw broke, but nothing came out. Nothing could release the pain. Just ridiculously crawling onto the floor, constantly bawling my eyes out. No matter how much I train myself to not care or feel anything. My mother is always there to remind me that I can still feel terrified, or despondent.

Chapter 11

Dan

"Come on Dan. I'm here to pick you up."

A voice woke me up in my bed. He sounded familiar.

"Hey, are you coming or what? What are we waiting for?"

I slide out of bed.

"We're leaving town. For good this time. But we have to go now."

But I haven't packed. My black bag appeared on my lap, but there was nothing inside but a shampoo bottle. I think it's a shampoo bottle although I'm unable to read the label.

"Come on son. Before your mother gets back."

Dad?

I leapt out of bed. The urge to run down the stairs washed over me. I wanted to flee at the highest speed, as fast as my scrawny legs will allow. But the legs seemed to only take short heavy strides as if gravity was turned up by ten. It was as if there were weights planted into my trainers.

"Don't you want to come with me?"

More than anything. Hold on for a minute. Just don't leave without me. Please. Please. Don't go. I'll go with you anywhere.

That's what I wanted to say, but I couldn't speak. Too busy grinding my teeth caused by the agony of lifting my own weight.

Suddenly, I'm no longer at home. Not standing in my tiny mid-terrace, but now based underneath a doorless wooden frame.

Where am I?

Everything's in black and white: me, the sand, the pier, the rails, and the sea. *I'm at the beach.*

Not just any normal beach—a very vacant beach, no one in sight for miles. There's no sound. In fact, there's no wind.

I've been here before.

Yes. It's the same beach I and Joe used to go to.

But where are all the people? Where is the wind? Why's there such an anomalous silence?

I look up to view a trio of seagulls, circling the air like vultures. Some lumps of sand were pulsating. A clown appears in front of me. Though not a happy clown, his big red smile was long gone. The make-up was drawn to replicate a pumpkin's evil grin and its sharp triangular eyes.

Both of the clown's hands were flapping. No, not flapping. They're shaking. His vibrating white gloves enter his sleeves. As I was expecting a bouquet of flowers to magically appear, I was surprised to see a collection of pumpkin leaves trickle to the ground. They were to feed his black horse. The stallion did not eat any of the treats. The clown just held its finger against its snout, ordering the steed to be quiet. When the dark horse's master opened his mouth, I watched as all his teeth fell out. In the blink of an eye, the entertainer and his pet disappeared. I could hear the waves of the ocean. It diverted my expressionless attention towards the thinnest ripples of water. As the tide pulled out from the fresh sand it left a damp patch, darkening the brightest of grains. This time a waft of salty seawater left more than clammy sand. It left a thing most people would be traumatised by. But I am not most people. I can see my own emotionless body as if I am viewing myself from outside of my own body. I know that I should have been terrified by the dead corpse the shore brought unsuspectingly. Somehow, I knew that it was going to happen. Honestly, it needed to happen.

The water now flowed around the body as if Mother Nature herself can never cover up this shameful truth.

However, the carcass has no face. It's been peeled off. Perhaps, it's yet to have been given one. The body itself has been brutally stabbed, repeatedly. I would say it happened to someone who must have deserved it. A detective would say it's a crime of passion. Meaning, it was someone who I know.

Chapter 12

Dan

Are we defined by our mothers? I hope not. What would that make me? Some kind of monster? What are monsters? They are not furry monsters with horns or fangs. Just uncaring people who consciously make bad decisions. These are the thoughts circulating my mind whilst loading the washing machine.

After the nightmare, I woke up in sheets drenched in cold sweat and urine. Embarrassed by such a childish flaw, I told my mum it was a wet dream. Another lie. I'm getting good at those. I suppose we all have to be good at something.

I never had a wet dream. My libido is close to non-existent. It's not that I find the act of sex repulsive, it's just something that doesn't cross my mind. However, my counterpart (Joe) is the complete opposite. I'm sure he would rather walk Gemma home than me. Am I holding him back? Maybe he's better off without me?

I lost my line of thought as I fell into a deep hypnotic state caused by the sheets spinning around the old washing machine. The endless cycling of white linen spun round on a loop. I could swear I've just seen a red ink dot on one of the sheets.

Have I left a pink sock in by mistake?

The wet soapy sheet with a red smidge is now stuck on the clear-view visor, whilst the pillowcases and the duvet covers are still spinning behind. The red blot on the sheet is growing and growing, forming different shapes and patterns.

This can't be happening.

The whole sheet is now entirely red. The single mattress sheet now peels off the window and all I can see is thick red blood spinning round and round.

Crashing like waves against the rotating inner drum. Contaminating all the bed sheets with blood.

Cream Beetle. The smell of smoke and mould killer. Deep breaths. Brown cardboard. The memory of you and Joe, using Christmas wrapping paper for Lightsabre fights. The annoying sound of bass coming from the house opposite the road. Blue bins. The rough edges of brick scratching my hands.

A little trick I learned to help with anxiety, called the '*Five-four-three-two-one Grounding Technique*'. I merely shortened it a tad. Take some slow steady breaths to regain my posture and hold on to reality. What I saw there was not real. The sheets were white and will come out white.

There is no desire to see anybody hurt. My heart rate is now coming down. I felt the presence of someone watching. It was my neighbour, Neil. Short guy, glasses and a bald head. Once I gave eye contact, he turned away awkwardly. That's all he ever does—'look the other way'. Through the thin walls, he could always hear my cries for help when my mum beat me. Still, the weakling did nothing about it.

A line of school kids queue up at the entrance of the school. A new beep sound echoes down the halls.

"I've been petitioning for a metal detector to the headmaster for years, but he never listened. Of course, it takes one dead kid, to make him aware."

One snooping teacher told the other, while she smokes.

My pace to the school was like a napping tortoise's. I feel like attending school is now just a pointless exercise. The queue was long and had far too many people. I noticed some of the other schoolboys sneaking off. Probably because they didn't want their lighters, or 'protection', to be confiscated. I followed them.

For the first time, I 'skived'. Wandering down an empty estate, I crept past the pub where Joe's mum works. She only does late shifts so I shouldn't see her. In the middle of the road is a crow picking on the scraps of someone's spilt pile of takeaway chips. Its dark and empty eyes gazed upon me. Threatened by the chance I'd be stealing its meal, it cawed defensively.

Desby's football hooligan club, 'Desby-Does-em'. *A ridiculous title.* The overweight fighters were plodding their way to the watering hole. To complete the quest for more stale, piss-poor lager, and crisps.

I forgot they were playing at home today.

They stopped jabbering midway through their conversations to give me their icy stares. Inspecting to see if I was a scout from a rival team. I can still feel them leering their aggressive eyes at my bony back while I walk past. My knee wants to wobble. My lungs are gasping for air.

Why can't people see that I crave to be left alone?

It infuriates me. You try your best to do what's right in the world, and then other people out there just want to hurt you. I'm forever torn between wanting to do good, and the need to raise my defences to fight others away. It's enough to crack the mind in two.

I placed myself on a park bench and began to write. Writing helps clear my mind and regain some control. Right now there's a whirlwind of negative convictions trying to escape my broken mind. Regretting not taking my coat, the cold winter's wind brings a chill to the bones.

"What *ya* writing there?"

An unfamiliar voice arises from in front. Some girl had parked herself up on the opposite side of the bench without the courtesy of asking for permission. With not being in the mood to start a conversation, I face up to oust her. As I was about to speak some unwarranted obscenities. Suddenly, I was left dumbfounded by a pretty face and dark eyes.

She combed the matching black hair over the large, hooped earrings exposing her immaculate cheekbones. The longer I stared at her the more I debated whether the earrings actually suited her. However, I am fond of the one streak of dyed red hair. It dawned on me that I've been gawking at her longer than I intended.

Ow.

"I said 'What are you writing?'"

"Did you just kick me?"

I peep under the table to see her black leggings and bright white pumps.

Ow.

"You've just done it again!"

"You're not answering my question."

"Why would I tell you?"

"Because I'll kick you again if you don't."

Her smile was arrogant. God, this girl is so annoying.

"I'm writing a poem."

There was a hint of shame in my tone.

"Why do you sound so embarrassed about it?"

"Because the last time I read any of my poems, it was to my best friend, and I just got called gay."

"It depends. Is your best friend a girl?"

"No, he's called Joe."

"That's why he called you gay. Let's have a look."

She leapt over the bench table and took my scribblings without permission.

"It's good."

"It's not, you're just saying that to be polite."

"No, I mean it. Better than anything I could ever do."

I couldn't help but release a bashful smile.

"You should smile more, then you wouldn't look so fucking depressed."

"I get that… a lot."

"You should also gel your hair, get rid of that cowlick. Plus, it'll make you look more handsome. You don't talk much do you?"

I was just about to reply when—

"Why aren't you in school? You're in uniform. Playing hookie?"

She cackled.

I couldn't think of an excuse. Not one that didn't sound so depressing. Mentioning any relations to negative emotions instantly puts folk off.

"You're a bad boy aren't you?"

She tilts her head and bats a flirtatious, but playful grin.

"I do quite like a bad boy."

I begin to fidget on my seat and rub my hands awkwardly.

"I'm not really bad at all."

"I get it. You're a clever, moody, I-like-to-eat-lunch-on-my-own, quiet boy."

"You don't know me."

"I can read people. It's one of my many talents. I'm not just a pretty face."

"How old are you?"

"AH! Don't you know it's rude to ask a lady her age?"

"You don't go to my school?"

"I dropped school."

"Isn't your mum mad?"

"Oh yeah, she's furious. But she is a pretentious bitch, who needs to buy something new every time she's remotely sad. So. She. Can. Suck. It."

The awkwardness had dominated my nerves. However, my previous negative beliefs and any words in my vocabulary have faded away. Leaving me dumb.

"What about your dad?"

"I don't know who he is."

"You can join our No-dads-club."

She squints her dark eyes, unsure if she's puzzled or that I have offended her.

"What's the No-dads-club? Are you not letting whoever has a father figure in? Who's in it?"

"My best friend Joe, and me, lost our dads when we were little. It's actually how we met. His dad died in Iraq. But mine just walked out."

"Bastard."

"I hope you are referring to my dad, and not Joe's."

"It sucks, but at least you two found each other because of it."

"I never looked at it, in that way before."

"Let me sit next to you."

I was surprised. Does this girl actually like me? Skinny, socially awkward, depressing me?

There might have been a possibility…. In a different reality. When she stood up, I noticed a slight pregnant bump poking out her white tank top. An estimation of five months. I felt crushed. Supposedly, I was expecting disappointment. Someone as cool as her would not be interested in me.

She took out her hand.

"My name is Nicki Yakes."

'*Nicki Yakes*'. There was a lump in my throat, not due to being shy, but dread was sinking in. Victor Romeo's crew, Leebee and his gang, are looking for this girl. She's trouble, and she's probably going to get me killed. I panic.

"I have to go."

I grab all my notes and my belongings. Carelessly shoving them in my bag, crimping all my work.

"Wait, where are you going?"

"I-I-I… realise that I have to be somewhere, sorry."

I scurry away, repetitively looking back at her angry, yet stunning, expression. Once I fled away at a safe distance, I felt humiliated by my inability to maintain dignity, and for looking back. I never look back.

Chapter 13

Joe

"Sorry, kid, we're fully staffed. Not taking anyone on, anytime soon."

Bob's Cafe was the fourth place I had tried to get a job. Well, I bet the Polish Garage was taking on some apprentices. They said 'no' to me because I'm not Polish. I'm positive that's the reason. Nowadays, you can't say stuff like that. Too many snowflakes will accuse you of being racist.

The High Street is completely dead. It shouldn't be a ghost town on a Saturday morning. Nobody could be arsed to get off their backsides—they stay in and order online.

Walking down an alleyway, I'd noticed people are too idle to put their shit in the bins. Despite having wheelie bins outside everyone's back gates, there are bags of rubbish all over the floor. A rat legs it out of one of the split bags and heads to safety. I watch where my foot goes, and leap over peoples dribs and drabs. The smell is unbearable. If I open my mouth, I'm gonna puke on someone's wall.

How can people live like this? Why did I take this shortcut?

I saw an empty chips tray on the ground. It made me realise that there I was one place left to try… *McDonald's.* I don't wanna work there. It'll be so embarrassing. No, I can do better. Maybe if I study harder, I can get some better grades. But books are boring and the internet is too slow to watch any videos. *Sigh*. Don't know what I'm going to do. There is another job offer that is nagging at me. I can't really work for Leebee.

It'll be good money. Think of the things you could buy for you and your mum.

It'll be illegal.

Won't be forever. Just until you find something else.

I could get killed.

Could it get me killed?

Michael Clark pops into my head. His hand reaching out. Covered in blood. Dying in agony on the school field. Surrounded by so many other kids. No one cared enough to protect him. No one to have his back. No one to keep him safe.

"I don't want to die."

Those were his last words. Imagine those being your last words. Fuck. So whiney. So soft. So tragic. I had been thinking so hard, I didn't realise I was out of the alleyway. At least that wretched smell went.

Where am I naa?

A few blocks away from Archers Road…

Chapter 14

Dan

Snow is up to our heels. My uncle and I were trudging through the snow. The winter brings much snowfall to the north, especially the forest by Uncle Clive's farm. Despite the freezing temperature and my scrawny physique, we were both protected by our snow boots, hats, and thermals. I notice that Uncle Clive is a little bit slower than his normal self.

No one can win the battle against time, not even someone as headstrong as Uncle C. Old age will come for us all—it's not like we can revert to being young again. Dissimilar to the trees around us. The cold winter might take what life these skinny branches will grow, but in the summer their youthful glow will shine again.

"This is the spot."

My one and only uncle turn around to look me in the eye. The cold air makes his heavy gasping visible. His wrinkly face is pale, and his bushy grey beard has trapped floating remnants of snow. I use the gloves to load the licensed shotgun.

"Are you sure about this?"

There was a quiver in my voice.

"I'm certain."

I feel regret swim within my body.

"There should be plenty of deer around here," He bellowed.

We'll be very surprised to get deer in our proximity. Uncle C is not the most discreet person.

"You could go to a supermarket, like any other normal person."

"Where's the fun in that?"

He releases a roaring belly laugh like *Brian Blessed* in *Flash Gordon.*

"I'm really sorry to hear about that Michael Park fella."

"It's Clark," I corrected.

"Well, poor son-of-a-bitch shouldn't have had his life taken away from him so early. His poor mother and father, having to bury their son so soon. With his whole life ahead of him. It makes me sick! Sick! I tell ya."

My Uncle Clive makes an unusual grunt when he's angry.

"I was going to ask if I could leave early tomorrow morning? There is a service for Michael tomorrow morning. I was hoping to attend."

"No problem, son."

Me and my hunting partner crouch to take cover against a fallen log. Now that we're stationary I can start to feel the cold on my face.

"Have you popped your cherry yet?"

Embarrassment brought some colour back into my cheeks.

"Uncle Clive."

"Well, have you got a girlfriend yet?"

"Not yet. I haven't met anyone whom I fancy."

"*Ooh… 'hom I fancy'… la-dee-da.* You definitely got the brains from my son. I just wish he wasn't such a self-centred arsehole. Leaving you and your mum like that. I'll give him a black eye if I ever see that piece of shit again."

This is a topic I'm not overly fond of. Yes, Clive is actually my Grandfather, but he prefers 'Uncle'. According to him, it makes him sound 'less old'.

"How is your psycho-bitch of a mother?"

Still not one for sugar-coating, are you?

"My mum still has her ups and downs. The hallucinations are appearing worse. She doesn't hit me as much though."

"It's no excuse. I told you, you should have lived with me."

"My mum kept saying 'I need you to take care of me'. Every time I tried to leave, she would start crying. That was then."

"How do you feel now?"

"She can get fucked."

"Good man, people who use emotional blackmail to control others, deserve to be on their own."

My Uncle pulled a smile that meant he was more than proud. But I don't feel proud of it. It felt necessary, for my own sanity.

"Consider moving in. Help me with my land, until you get into college."

Believe me, I have.

As my uncle creeps up over the log, he whispers,
"There's a deer. My boy."

Emerging gently over the log's surface, I spot a fallow deer. Its large furry body rests on the ground below. This creature could viciously attack us with its antlers, should I miss the shot. I squint to close the weakest eyelid. It's cute black eyes catch mine. Still, it does not move. Not even when I am aiming the barrel end of a shotgun directly at the mammal.

"Go on, you can do it. The safety's off, just pull the trigger," he whispered.

"Mind the recoil, Dan."

His long face knows that its opponent does not have the spine to do the job. I drop the weapon onto the floor. The buck retreats for protection.

My uncle frowns in disappointment. I was ashamed.

"What did you do that for?"

"I'm sorry, I just couldn't do it."

"It's okay to hold a shotgun and shoot animals. As long as you don't shoot anyone else."

I think I'd rather shoot another human than an innocent creature. Animals in the wild live in the dirt and kill others to survive. People are just dirty and kill each other because they can. Are we really the superior race?

"Come on, let's get you back home."

I sighed with relief when my Uncle said that. I can get back to reading Van Gogh's biography.

Chapter 15

Joe

Outside the boarded terraced street that was once Archers Road, is a patch of lumpy grass, where kids used to kick a ball against the graffitied wall. Leebee and his gang hang out on the green. I scanned the layout. Three of 'em are on the wall giggling and disrupting any peace by playing *Skepta*. I recognise them. They used to play at the Youth Centre after school. I guess this is where they ended up after the government stopped funding it. On the path, Leebee was staring at the *One Shop* in the working corner. One shady looking large bloke in a puffer jacket and carrying a grey duffel bag, walked out the shop, stuffing his fat face with more sweets. He waddled further up the road, then crouched to drop his sweet wrappers in the bin.

As I approached Leebee, a gigantic hand slapped my shoulder, pulling me back. Two bouncers blocked me in my tracks. Looking down at me with their suspecting eyes and raging faces.

"Wha' ya *tink* you gonna be doin' bruv?"

"I'm here to see Leebee."

"Get to fuck out of 'ere."

"Allow."

Leebee cleared. His eyes maintained on the bin near the park.

While my body was being patted down by gigantic hands, that'll leave a few bruises later. I went to see what fascinated Leebee, by returning my look to the shop, bin, and the puffer jacket guy.

There's something different about him?

Now he's further away, I have to squint to get a better view.

The bag! Where has the bag gone?

A skinny kid, not older than twelve sprinted out of the park, picked up the grey duffle bag from behind the bin, and took the package in the complete opposite direction to the puffer man. This seemed to please Leebee—the right kid must have done the pick-up.

They're using kids! It's wrong, and you know it!

The two gorillas finished patting me down for weapons. Then one pointed to their boss.

"Leebee, My name is Joe."

"The other day you said you had some work."

"Yeah, man."

He slapped my hand and wheeled me in, patting his hand on my back. I admit, it feels strange to be so welcomed.

"Don't mind those two. They'd be 'ere to protect us."

"When do I start? How does it work?"

I'm starting to feel nervous, I hope I'm not asking too many questions.

"Take *dis*."

Leebee pulls out a mobile phone from his pocket. Puts it into my hands. I had forgotten how heavy these old *Nokia's* were.

"Do ya see that boy, we the blue checked shirt? *Wid* me grey backpack?"

"Yeah."

Wonder where this is going?

"Follow the package to Craigson Avenue. Any problems, ya call the one number *dat's* in *der*."

I assume he's selling some drugs.

"He's just a kid."

Shit. Did I say that out loud?

66

Leebee dead eyes me, I've asked too much. He's gonna kill me.

"*Dat* boy's stepdad was beating him. He came to us. Now he be protected."

Might be wise not to ask about the stepdad.

"I'm sorry."

Don't apologise! You'll look weak.

"Ya understand whad'ya need to do?"

I nod, anxiously.

"Ya can keep *dat* burner for *t'ree* days, max. Our boy gets picked up by the pigs, ya dump that phone. Smash it, *t'row* it in *da* sewers. I don't care, just get rid."

Did he mention "The cops?"

Never thought about the police until now. I can't go to jail. I'm getting in over my head. My grip on the mobile is loosening caused by my sweaty palms.

"Ya best get started."

"What time do I… finish?"

"Till *da* bag's emptied."

My dry throat gulped. I started to run to catch up to the young lad.

Hey, isn't running a little suspicious?

That's a good point, I slowed down at the crossing to make it appear I was just running to the lights. Wish I could run or do any exercise. It would help with the nerves.

Chapter 16

Dan

The park at night has never been so occupied. A horde of mourners, and busybodies, gathered around one woman with curly hair, dressed in black. She wept on a piece of paper she clenched in her hands.

"Michael was kind, loving, caring…"

The agony within her was too much. No matter how prepared she was by writing down a eulogy. When it came to reading them out, Michael Clark's mother could not speak about the loss of her son. Hating herself for not being as strong as she would like to have been. Catherine's body began to shake.

"He was smart. Devoted. Passionate about *Call of Duty* and *Pokemon Cards.*"

There was a brief giggle from the nostalgic crowd.

"Above all those things, nothing could replace the love he had for his friends and family."

I stood by the fence away from the crowd. Although I had a few brief conversations with Michael, I wasn't worthy to stand at the front, to grieve with those who truly knew him. In fact, I didn't feel I was grieving, I barely knew him. I put myself out the way to remain unnoticed. It seemed to be a respectable choice. The drawback is that I can feel the grass's condensation is seeping through the holes in my trainers, and I could barely hear the spoken words.

"I don't wish to have a moment of silence for Michael's memory. I want you to listen to a song from his favourite band, *The National.*"

Michael's father, a neat, tall, thin figure, he knelt down on the grass, to pick up the Chinese lantern. Pulling a lighter from his pocket, you could tell he doesn't smoke, he attempted to light the centrepiece of the lantern.

"During the song; please, think about Michael. What he could have done in his future? His past achievements. The influences he had spread."

I didn't think of any of that. I enjoyed watching the inflated round balloon, brightening the starless, blackened sky. Gently floating across the sky, carrying its torch, to the gentle melodic strings of *The National's Start a War.*

Returning to Earth, I noticed a man was studying me. Someone tall, with thin round glasses, and a well-groomed dark beard. Now he was coming towards me. My shoulders became stiff. As he drew nearer, I recognised him. It was Gareth Hall, the new school psychologist.

What's he doing here?

"Hey, did you know the victim at all?"

"We attended school together. I never knew him well. Just wanted to pay my respects."

He knew I didn't know Michael well. A psychologist would detect that I'd be further into the crowd, in order to be closer to the deceased. He just wanted to have an opener. It's best to keep all my answers concise.

"What's your name?"

"Tom."

I lie to prevent my identity from being exposed.

"I'm Dr Gareth Hall. You can call me Gareth. It's still a mighty shame. Michael had his whole life ahead of him. There will be opportunities he shall never take, lovers he will not get to greet..."

For a moment, it appeared as if Gareth was sniffling.

Is he about to cry? Why would he cry? He's just moved here. He's never known Michael Clark.

He wiped a tear from his eye.

"Just imagine all the things he could have done in his life."

It's the mother and father I feel sorry for. Yes, Michael did have his whole life in front of him. Now, he's got out of this hell at peace. While the parents have to stay here. For the rest of their lives, they will have to live with the pain of losing a child. They will always be known as the couple whose child was murdered. Never to gain a new image ever again.

"What do you think happened?"

You know what happened. You're trying to analyse me, aren't you?

"This is how I perceived it: Michael Clark kept getting bullied by Joel Romeo. Michael started to take taekwondo, with my friend Joe. By all accounts, Mike got pretty good at it. Quite quickly. A born natural, as it were. One day, Michael had enough of Joel's bullying, so he challenged him to a fight in the schoolyard. Joel was unaware of Michael's new-found hobby and agreed to the fight. Michael expected a match that should be fair and square, nothing more. Michael was winning. This caused Joe to panic."

"So, he pulled out a knife."

"There's a reason why Joel panicked."

"Other than the fear of being humiliated in front of his peers?" Gareth probed.

"Joel had a reputation to maintain. One that pressured him to the brink of doing something too impulsive. His father is Victor Romeo," I stated.

Gareth recollected something from his mind, something he presumed would be trivial, until now.

"Isn't Victor Romeo the guy on the billboards? Those signs at the entrances of the newly developed estates in the next town over?"

"Yes, Victor Romeo is responsible for all the drugs flowing through Desby. Everybody knows it."

"Even the police?"

"No one seems to be able to find evidence against him. Some have tried."

"I think you have been watching too many films?"

I feel insulted that he is accusing me of being delusional. I form a credible excuse to vacate.

"I have to go home."

"It was nice talking to you."

I didn't respond. While I was treading on wet grass, disappearing into the night. Relaying my and Gareth's conversation, one thing I mentioned earlier lit up an observation. Joe was not present at his pals memorial. Where was he?

Chapter 17

Joe

Running my own corner today. Not far from Archers Road. I'm guessing that's where the new starters are tested. The backpack they gave is a lot lighter than I thought. Still there's so much weight. *So much responsibility.* I'm being carefully monitored by DC and his boys. He would love nothing more than to see me fail. Don't know why he doesn't like me. He just has something against me. As I turn to see his grim face, he whispers something into another bloke's ear. They both chuckled.

Bet he's talking about me. I just know it. I'm not in the mood for this. My eyes and drained body are shattered. I just want to go to bed or drop here on the cracked pavement. Last night the young blood didn't empty his *food* till three AM. Then, I got a call on the burner at seven—wi't someone telling me to be at work. Luckily, my mum was working nights at the club. I'm not sure how much more I'll get away with sneaking around. I don't want my mum to find out the truth—the news would kill her. That's the person I don't want to see get hurt.

Further down the road, Mikey waits with his hands in his hoodie. He's discarded his bright red hat and flashy white trainers to make him look less conspicuous. He's wearing something dull like me—a blue polo top, plain jeans and brown trainers. Mikey is approached by some shabby customers. They may dress as if they're homeless, with their baggy clothes, ageing faces, overgrown beards and breaking skin.

They even act homeless, constantly begging on the streets, telling young kids different stories every day: *'I need to get a train to Kings Cross' or 'I just missed the bus, can you help me out?'* Trying to get people to feel sorry for them. The truth is there's six of them squatting in a flat and getting smacked off their tits. I don't pity any of the leeches—they should spend money on actual FOOD rather than meth.

A skinny, scruffy-looking couple, who are both wearing coats twice their size, shuffle suspiciously towards me. The man is constantly scratching his patchy cheek. The scraggy woman talks harshly, having the roughest of throats.

"Alright love. How much for Tina?"

That was straightforward.

"Forty-two."

I stand for what feels like an eternity while they're coppering up their collection of change.

"We got forty? Will that do?"

I don't know much about the game, but I have a strong feeling, if I don't return with the correct count, Leebee and his crew wouldn't take kindly to it. DC would, he'd love to beat it out of me.

"No, sorry, it's got to be forty-two."

Shit, did I just say sorry?

"We'll bring back the other two quid tomorrow. I promise."

"No. I can't do that, I'm afraid."

"We're totally good for it. Honest."

I wouldn't trust them with a paperclip. Still, I was brought up on manners and I try to be as polite as possible.

"Please come back later, with the remaining two pounds, and then you can have your *food*."

"Please. Please. We'll come back tomorrow I swear."

Slowly losing my patience, here.

"No. I can't."

"Just give me a bag man."

He puts his dirty hand on my shoulder. I shrug it off.

"Guys, I'm going to have to ask you to leave."

"Dude, we're really good for it."

The man pleads, "We'll give you five quid tomorrow."

"No."

"Just give me a hit!"

Their tone was going from civilised to threatening. I can feel a rage bubbling in my stomach. I would love nothing more than to *hit* them.

"Just sell us it for forty. We had to spend some of the money on food, you see. We were so hungry."

"Oh so, hungry. See we're homeless," the man contributed, putting on a sad face.

There and then, I thought they were going to drop on their knees and beg. Everything was interrupted by the sound of the sirens.

No, not the pigs.

The junkies put on their hoods and stepped off. DC and his gang departed their separate ways, casually. I froze still.

What do I do?

Flashing blue warning lights circulated the area. As I watched the boys in blue step out of their vehicle. My heart leapt in my mouth, while a million thoughts passed so quickly, I couldn't gather a full sentence.

They've come for me. They're going to send me to jail! I can't go to jail! I'm gonna get beat up. Raped. I can't do it. I can't—

They put the cuffs on Mickey. Bent him over the hood. Tossed him in the back of the car.

Shit. Shit. I'm next.

The policemen return to the vehicle and start their engines. The car slowly creeps up towards me. I can't breathe. The shaking in my legs returned, I just wanna run, but I don't, it'll be too suspicious. I steadily turn to walk the other way. Keeping my head down so they won't recognise my face. No matter how much I plod, the car is edging nearer, and nearer. The rim of the police car is tailing me, inches away from my back. Soon we'll be in line with each other. The sirens are an ongoing ringing in my ears. If I use my hands to seal my ears, the constant sound will still worm its way inside. My body is shut down. The heavy footing is the only thing I can concentrate on. In the corner of my eye, I spot the rozzers' faces, twisting to investigate me.

73

They're going to stop and pull me over.

I've never been so small and stiff. I'm sure the little bit of brown from my skin has gone. The vehicle drove away. Now my heart is beating again, fast. I can breathe again. The feeling of fear has now gone, replaced by some new-found adrenaline.

The fear of getting caught was terrifying but getting away with it was… fun. I grinned. Colour is returning to my body. It was a rush. A healthier rush than what some of my customers will get. So it's okay for me to do it again.

Chapter 18

Joe

After escaping from the cops; I rang Leebee on the one number on the phone. He told me where to meet next, on a completely different street, late at night. Forcing me to miss Michael Clark's wake earlier.

"Wogone."

That's not a word I have the right to share. So I said a simple "Hey."

"What's up?"

"Mikey has been picked up by the police."

I told him straight. Leebee looked deeply concerned. He needed a minute to sketch a new plan.

"Did you destroy that burner?"

"Not yet."

"Do it now."

I followed the order. I dropped the *Nokia* down the nearest drain. Letting the dirty sewer water gulp up any evidence.

"Tomorrow night meet me on the High Street. A public meet. Outside *dat* takeaway. I'll drop ya a new contact n' ya wad."

Wait. I'm actually gonna get paid tomorrow? Awesome. I thought I'd have to wait another month or something.

"Then we both go inside and order some food."

"What type of food?"

I had to ask. With so much going on, I thought it best to be more specific.

"Chips. Burgers. Who gives a shit?"

That's not really good for my diet.

"Tomorrow at eight. Be there."

I was about to leave when—

"You did well today."

When Leebee said that, I felt a sense of satisfaction. Like, I've gained someone's approval, one that needed to be earned from an older, male, and respectable figure.

"Leebee, why did the cops pick up Mikey? Not me?"

"Prolly cause your ass is white."

"I thought racial profiling was an American thing."

"Let me school you. There's only one *t'ing* you white boys see, *dat's* colour."

"I'm not like that," I assured him.

"Ya gonna be a good soldier, Joe. Ya smart."

I was pleased to hear someone saying I was smart. Most people compare me to Dan. Everyone's an idiot compared to him. It's good to not feel so stupid for once.

Chapter 19

Dan

Can't avoid school any longer. It's getting close to my exams. Sitting in my usual front seat, I pretend to enjoy Mr Ford's lesson on the periodic table. The fool doesn't know that my photographic memory had it imprinted in my mind long ago. Nonetheless, I play the part of a good student. I need to pass them in order to get to sixth form, succeeded by a university that is out of this town. Particularly, if I want to gain a good job and remain out of the borders of Desby. I am expecting Joe to be at the same speed. I am worried that he is unable to keep at the same level. Or childhood vow means we need to leave for further education together. My musings of Joe distracted me from the lesson. I rotate my body to look upon my best friend, at the back of the class. I noticed the hefty bags underneath his slumping baby blue eyes. He appears to have not slept during the weekend. Studying all night, perchance? He's not asked for any tutoring for a while, so it could be plausible.

It's more than likely to be an all-night session on the Xbox, Dan.

Mr Ford was under the illusion that he could grasp the attention of the restless class. He stood in front of the study group, to make an announcement.

"We're going to look at human anatomy."
The class stopped gossiping among their peers, to read the books that Mr Ford slammed onto our desks.
"Turn to page three."
I followed his instructions, to see a picture of a naked man.
The children giggled at the penis.
I wondered why they didn't show his face.

77

Mr Ford babbled on, how the stomach is attached to the duodenum, then to the jejunum. Illium. Ascending colon. *Blah blah.*

Mere basics. How dull. Deciding to doodle, or 'take notes', I grabbed my pencil case for the different coloured pens.

The dreary presentation went on.

I scribbled onto the notebook.

The girl beside me screamed.

Everyone paused to wonder what the high-pitched wail was for. Her face looked at me as if I had grown an extra four heads, and boobs.

I was perplexed as to why she looked at me with such disconcerting eyes. As if I was the star attraction at the freak show. I soon noticed that my red pencil was digging into the page of the science book. My agitated pupils peered down to see what I had been drawing. My hands shook, dropping whatever I held. The naked man in the book was covered in waves of red scribbled blood, caused by the blue knife drawn into his stomach. An acute drawing of a long purple bowel seeped out from the large incision that was made in the fat man's stomach.

Chapter 20

Dan

Four expressionless green walls are soon to be replaced with padded ones. Where else will I be sent? Freaks like me need to be locked away, incarcerated. Hidden from society for their protection. Perhaps my own protection? It'll stop me from becoming a monster. This does not mean the end for me. It is a mere disheartening chapter. People's 'stories' don't have any closure. Life itself is no fairy-tale. There are no happy endings—it only ends with death. At this moment in time, I'm not sure if I care about myself, or whatever happens to me.

The mixture of apathy and the miserable ponderings leaves me slouching on the dull grey table, tapping my fingers towards the vacant chair opposite, appearing to be a common simpleton.

I regain my posture when Gareth enters the room.

About time. Let's get this over with.

He looks to be holding a folder. My school photo is on the front.

Is that my life? In that minuscule four-page folder?

Goes to show how insignificant my existence is.

"Hello. *Daniel Suddlemire.*"

The psychiatrist purposely overemphasised my name. Suppose he hasn't forgotten that I introduced myself as *Tom* when we first met.

"Would you mind if I record this?"

"Go ahead."

I felt obliged to agree as he already mounted the recorder on the desk. Nonetheless, consent is supposed to give me the feeling of being autonomous, in hope of giving me a sense of empowerment. It may be effective on morons, but not me.

Dr Hall leaned over the table to speak clearly in the Dictaphone.

"My name is Gareth Hall, and I am in the room with Daniel Suddlemire. Today's date is Monday the 3rd of December 2018. I brought Daniel here for an informal chat, regarding a picture he drew in class. Please see the uploaded image under the user's name."

'Informal chat'. Those words feel inappropriate given the situation and the recorder on the table.

Comparing Gareth's body language, he wants to give the impression of being open and having a sympathetic ear. By not folding his arms, leaning back, giving eye contact and lowering his shoulders. Whilst I remain the complete opposite. Gareth probably notices because he's studying me as well.

"Would you like to tell me about the graphic drawing?"

It's not a comic book.

"I didn't know I was doing it."
"I see."

He just said that to display active listening.

"I know why you've brought me here."
"You do?"

He raises his right thick eyebrow.

"I haven't killed anyone. I have no desire to hurt anyone."

"I believe you haven't killed anyone. Were you there when your pal Michael Clark was stabbed on the playground?"

"I never witnessed the actual stabbing, but I did see him… lying on the ground."

"It must have been traumatising, witnessing something like that?"

"I'm not sure how I feel about it."

"What makes you say that?"

"I don't know how I feel anymore."

My eyes are starting to burn.

"Do you have any problems with anxiety?"

I wanted to admit I did—it felt like a safe place. But I remain silent, for I don't know this person.

"People with anxiety, or depression, often find that their feelings don't belong to them. They tell themselves that 'they don't care'. When in fact, they do care, they actually care a great deal."

Gareth has piqued my interest. I'm starting to relate to what he says.

"Why would someone do that?"

"Mainly to protect themselves from getting hurt. However, emotions can't be suppressed forever. They'll seep out eventually. Hence your drawing. Do you feel angry about Michael's death?"

"I suppose I do, he didn't deserve to die like that. Maybe he would have had a better chance if he wasn't in this town."

"Do you see images of his death? Do you feel like you want to hurt the person that did it?"

"I have been seeing images of blood. I have been experiencing some nightmares. I am so angry, and I am scared. All the time."

A tear rolls down my cheek. Even if I've exposed my weakness, a weight has been lifted. It felt good to tell someone. Now I can breathe again.

"What are you scared of?"

Everyone.

"What if someone else stabs me? It could be walking home from school, and a gang could just attack me. I've been having panic attacks before I leave the house. Holding my breath whilst I walk past a group of people. The one place where I should be safe has got my mum in it."

"Your mum? Does she not make you feel safe?"

I'm worried I've opened a can of worms here.
"She used to hit me when I was smaller. Not so much now. She's an alcoholic, torturing me with emotional, and psychical abuse."

Gareth couldn't hide his calm facade any longer. His face was furious, his breathing was deeper, and he clenched a fist. Which is unusual for a professional to do.

"Have you ever reported your mum to child services? Or tried to leave?"

"In the past, I've tried to run away, but she ends up crying, pleading on her knees, telling me that she needs me. Insisting that I stay, to help battle her disease."

"That's a lot of pressure on such a young man."

"It was. Now, I just want to leave her, and this town for good."

Gareth smiled, as he opened the folder on his desk.

"You are a very educated person, Daniel. You are expecting to receive the highest grades in your upcoming exams. I shouldn't say this, but you have been accepted in all the colleges and sixth forms you have applied for. I noticed you did not apply to Desby College. I can't say I blame you—it has failed the Ofsted inspection for a third year."

"I have to get out of this town. I feel so increasingly unhappy here."

Gareth leaned forward with intent.

"Are you bored at this school? Do you find the work unchallenging? Do you often get distracted easily?"

"Yes. To all those questions."

"I can't work out if it's because of your depression, or your high IQ? I think it could be both of those attributes."

Gareth pulls out a leaflet, from the file.

"Take a look at this school."

I stare inquisitively at a photo of a long road, leading to a cream mansion, resting behind neatly trimmed hedges.

"What is it?"

"That is a school for minds such as yourself. Fellow pupils, with roughly the same amount of intelligence. It is your ticket out of here. I can get you an application form. Providing you get the expected grades in the springtime, which I'm sure you will, you'll start in the new semester in September."

"Where is it?"

"Hampshire."

"That will be a long commute."

"There will be student accommodation provided."

Joe! What about the pact you made with Joe?

"Could I take someone with me?"

This question could persuade Gareth to change his mind.

"It would depend. It would definitely cost more. It would have to be a spouse—"

"Brother?" I interrupted.

"I can see what I can do. However, this opportunity won't be available so easily. There is something I need you to do."

A drawback is approaching. I knew it sounded too good to be true.

"I need you to see me on a weekly basis. I have to see real improvement from you…"

Improvement from *me?*

"Until those visions in your head are gone."

"I know what you mean. You want to know if it's safe enough to let me loose in society."

I caught Gareth by surprise.

"Have you ever considered joining a social group? A local football team, perhaps?"

"I'd rather go skinny dipping in the Arctic Ocean."

Gareth tried to hide his chuckle.

I was starting to get excited about the idea. Stuffing the leaflet in my pocket, a feeling of dread boiled in my stomach.

"Why would you want to help me?"

The doctor leaned back, deeply reflecting on the past.

"I had this one boy in my care that refused to eat anything. So skinny, you could see all his waistline, even his ribs. He suffered from anorexia, causing him to be so tired, fragile, and pale. But you know what he said to me? He said 'No fat, no chemicals, that I've consumed will stimulate, or affect my mind and emotions'. He looked in my eyes and said, 'I am perfection'."

Despite it being a sad tale, what did it have to do with me? I'm guessing, by the sullen face, he has lost a patient once. Probably sworn an oath to save as many kids as he can. Gareth breaks a psychologist's golden rule—don't get too personally involved.

Chapter 21

Joe

The text from Dan said to be at the school gates for six. It's now nearly half-past. Hope he's alright—he really scared us in class. Bitches like Connie kept saying he's a freak. I tell em, that he wouldn't hurt anyone if he tried. But, I don't know how long I can stick up for him. He's really gonna have to stand up for himself now. Maybe I'll drag him to next week's boxing class. My first one today was a lot different from taekwondo—my shoulders and arms never ached so much. The *el-dolphins* have really kicked in though. That's not right—endorphins, that's what I meant. I'm so pumped, I don't care.

"Joe, thanks for meeting me."

Dans' voice caught me by surprise. Making me jump out of my skin.

"Hey, buddy, how's it going?"

I know I'm concerned, but I didn't mean to sound so patronising.

"I have some good news," he smiled.

He showed me a leaflet of a right posh school.

"Take a look and see what you think," he urged.

"What's it meant to be?"

"It's our ticket out of here. It's one of those schools for the gifted. The school's psychologist, Gareth, said he can get me a place."

He said 'me'. Is he gonna ditch me, and leave? I've never seen him so excited, not in a long time. I can't deny his wishes, but we made a promise. Maybe he's forgotten about the day on the beach. It was a long time ago.

"Is this what you really want?"

"You're coming with me."

I was wrong.

"What would I do, while you're doing these smart courses, and hanging out with your new posh friends?"

His face sunk. It's obviously something Dan never thought of.

"Take a look at the brochure. See if there's something you can do."

I open up the booklet to read. I can't read any of the information. My dyslexia makes it hard to concentrate, and it's even worse when Dan's wide eyes are pressuring me to. So I make an excuse.

"I'll take it home and read it."

I'm not going to read it. It would be pointless; I won't get the grades. Can't see me at some posh school, studying shit that I'll never get. I changed the topic.

"You need to defend yoursen'."

Dan looks confused.

"What do you mean?"

"People *tink* you're a weirdo, especially after today."

"Did you say 'tink' rather than think?"

I must have picked it up from Leebee and his boys. Dan stares at me with a real dazed look. Is he judging me? He has no right to! Still, best not tell him about my new job. He'd go mental, probably tell my mum to stop me n'all. Dan would swallow his pride to protect me, but I don't need protecting.

"Don't matter about dat."

Did I just say 'dat' instead of 'that'?

"Dan, I'm going to teach you how to box."

His face looked disgusted.

"When did you learn the art of boxing?"

"I took my first lesson today. Just form a fist."

I take my defensive stance, protecting my face with my fists. Placing my stronger side back.

"Why do I need to do this?"

"Just do it."

I lightly jab him in his puny right arm.

"I don't want to fight you, mate."

"Just form a fist, otherwise I'll keep hitting you."

He sighed. Eventually, Dan did what I asked, but with very little enthusiasm.

"Not like that. You'll break your thumb."

Amateur.

"Why do you care about something as trivial as boxing? It's such a primitive sport, encouraging violence and the pain of others. While the millionaires make money from the lower classes' misfortune."

I jab his skinny body some more. Now, he raised his arms for protection.

"Why are you avoiding looking at the brochure? It's our chance to escape."

"It's *your* chance."

I punch a little harder. He blocks my shots.

"You know I can't leave without you, Joe."

"It sounds like I'm holding you back."

I dug into his lower body. I was impressed when he dodged the attack.

"You're not holding me back. Believe me when I say that I envisaged myself, stopping you from reaching your full potential."

He takes a swing at me this time. I laugh at his failure.

"Is it because you're anxious about the academic side?"

Something inside me snapped. I felt so guilty when I fully pelted Dan in his nose.

He moans on the floor. I lean over to apologise.

"Dan! I'm so sorry. Are you okay?"

"Get away from me."

He pushes me away with one hand, the other hand. The other is holding his bloody nose.

"I think you broke my nose."

"I'm really sorry, I didn't mean to."

I helped him to his feet. I shouldn't have tried fighting him. I forgot how sensitive Dan was when we were younger. He'd cry if I hurt him too much while play-wrestling.

"It's okay. Best I go home to clean my wound."

I was relieved when he forgave me. Dan also reminded me I too needed to shoot off to meet Leebee.

"Sorry, Dan. Are you okay getting home?"

"Yeah, I'll be fine."

It sounds selfish, but I was pleased I didn't have to escort him home.

"Brothers, yeah?"

"Yes, we still are brothers."

We hugged it out. I told Dan to text me when he gets in. I hope the next time I see Dan, he'll have forgotten about this fancy school thing.

Chapter 22

Dan

Betrayal. That's what it felt like when Joe punched me in the face. The ache from my throbbing nose doesn't make me want to cry, it was the disloyalty. I am struggling to conceive that he hit me. What was running through his mind? He had one boxing lesson, now he believes he is *Muhammad Ali.*

At least he apologised.

I gaze upon the dry blood staining my pale palms.

Anyone can make an empty apology. The two simple words—'I'm sorry' can't cover everything.

"I'm sorry that I've used your pocket money to get drunk" ... "I'm sorry that me and my friends jumped you and took your mobile" ... "I'm sorry that I stabbed your son to death, Mr and Mrs Clark."

One word cannot bring redemption. People are vile, merciless, and are stupid to conceive that consequences aren't real. That it's a mere concept.

I recalled the times myself and Joe have fought or argued. It was always me who would make the first apology, even when it was never my fault. I am not one for arguing, or fighting, it would break me into tears. I'm glad to have a tougher exterior now.

Despite still avoiding conflict, I am no longer going to repent for an act that I have not caused. Not going to let my opponent see me cry. Notwithstanding, if myself, or Joe, was backed into a corner. I would do whatever needs doing to save us. Whatever it takes.

The walk home seems much longer. I am not sure how much more I can withstand the pain. It's not like I can knock on a stranger's door and ask for their help. There's no one to turn to. No one I can trust to help me.

"Hey, cutie. You're not going to run away from me again, are you?"

A familiar friendly voice cropped up from behind my shoulder. It was Nikki Yakes. Best escape before that pretty face seduces me into some kind of trouble.

Nikki grabbed my shoulder. Yanked me back. Then stood in front of me, blocking my escape. Surprisingly able for a pregnant woman. Her arms were crossed, her kind face was displeased. Underneath her pointy eyebrows, her dark eyes pierced right through my quivering body.

"Are you ignoring me too?"

"No, I—I—"

'I—I' had been caught dead-to-rights. For I was running away. I believed my runner's legs would outpace her wobbling. Now I'm left speechless, shuffling my head awkwardly to avoid eye contact with her wild ones.

"You're bleeding."

Suddenly, she stopped being furious. A natural mothering instinct kicked in when she saw I was hurt.

"Let me have a look."

She gently touched the end of my red nose, causing me to flinch with pain.

"What happened?"

I was about to answer but was interrupted.

"Did you get in a fight? I knew you were a bad boy. First skiving school, and now I find out you're a fighter. You really are a dark horse. I'd hate to see the other guy, right?"

"My best friend accidentally punched me."

I sounded so meek.

She put her hands on her hips and flared a look of disapproval.

"How can your best friend 'accidentally' punch you? If you ask me, he sounds like a rubbish friend. That's the thing with friends, they always leave you in the end."

She now imitates a sarcastic, high pitch 'girly girl' voice, mocking the stereotype. *We're totes gonna always be BFF.* ... "*Yeaaah Girrrrrl-frrrriend.*" ... "*It's us bitches together, we ain't gonna let no man come between us.*"

I hated it when the smile from her kind face disintegrated.

"As soon as you get pregnant; the word 'mate' soon gets replaced with 'slag'. Then they don't want *nowt* to do with you."

"I'm sorry to hear that."

I actually felt pitiful. But when I spoke out loud, I wasn't sure if it came across as sympathetic, or as a robot on the autocue.

She gave a sparkling white smile. I knew it was an act. I too had to pose fake smiles to fellow pupils, teachers, Joe, and my mother.

"Hey, it's not your problem, right?"

I guess not.

"I live around the corner from here. Why don't you come back to mine, and I'll fix you up?"

I knew full well I shouldn't go. There was a part of me that really wanted to follow where she led. A kaleidoscope of winged insects swarmed around my stomach. Intertwining with each other in a figure of eight, forming a knot—one that grew tighter as I approached her house.

Her semi-detached was on the bottom of a hill. The front side door was above a few steps. When I'm in public and anxious, I tend to observe my surroundings—it's like a neurotic twitch. One car stood out amongst the others, due to its shiny and flashy appearance. It was a bright red *Toyota Camry.* I can't be certain because of the low sun blinding my eyes, but I think there is someone inside.

"Can you take your shoes off?"

Nikki's request broke my fixation on the vehicle. I stepped inside.

A girl's bedroom was like how I imagined: cut-outs of handsome vampires, and band members with jet black hair, and eyeliner, stuck on the peachy walls. Clothes were discarded all over the floor despite having a very wide wardrobe. I sat rigidly on the edge of a white makeup chair. My narrow legs were too close together, and I couldn't stop rubbing my palms together.

I had never been to a girl's bedroom before, I hope my mum doesn't find out.

You're in a pretty girls bedroom, and the only thing that is in your mind is your mother. This is a worrying quirk.

Nikki returns with a bowl of water and a cloth, placing it on the cosmetics desk, before sitting down on her bed, facing me.

She looks me straight in the eyes before divulging the bad news.

89

"This is going to hurt."

Her serious eyes divert towards the source of my anguish, the broken nose.

"Are you ready?" she warned.

"For what?"

Click.

I use her pillow to muffle the sound of screaming. I rock back and forth from the chair, bellowing in agony.

Nikki is giggling at my suffering.

"It serves you right."

"Why does it?" I cried.

"For running away from me. You still haven't explained yourself. Don't think that I've forgotten because I haven't. You're not leaving here until you explain yourself. So, go on. Speak. Justify yourself. Now."

Her tone is demanding, but Nikki's generosity proved that she deserves an explanation.

"Me, and my friend Joe—"

"Your best friend, who punched you. Yes, you've told me about him."

Her interrupting is such a frustrating habit.

"We were both walking home one night. A car pulled up. Leebee and his gang stepped out. They asked us if we knew you."

"I see. And you're worried that I'd get you in trouble."

"I don't want to get caught up in something I am not supposed to."

"I understand. You don't need to worry, they got me. So if you wanna leave, then I don't blame you."

She lay on her bed, legs crossed, picking up her headphones, and started to unravel the spaghetti junction.

I know pursuing the situation would lead me to a path I couldn't return from. But I didn't want her to shut me out. I also want to stay in her room just a few minutes longer.

"What happened when they caught you?"

Her dark green, stabbing eyes leer at me.

"They didn't do anything to me. Well, nothing physically. They warned me."

A dreadful feeling sunk into my stomach, killing those fluttering butterflies.

"What did they warn you about?"

"If I tried running away again. Then they'd kill my mum."

An atmosphere fogged up in the room, one forming over my head. Creating a stillness in the air. Freezing me.

"They want my baby."

"Why do they want your baby?"

"Because of his father."

In a disturbing, overwhelming state, I dig my fingers into my head. The thick strands of hair slide in between my skinny fingers. Pressing the tips hard against the skull, in order to force out a reluctant question.

"Who is the father?"

Nikki inhaled deeply.

"The father is Joel Romeo… meaning the grandfather is Victor Romeo."

Chapter 23
Joe

I dug into the warmest, pale, and possibly worst tray of chips I've ever had. While sitting on the plastic chairs in the takeaway on the main street, Leebee slipped me an envelope under the table. It was surprisingly heavy. In the toilet stall, I view its contents. There was a *Samsung* phone so thick it could survive a nuclear blast. No charger? With these phones, it'll last a week without one. The thing that surprised me the most was a load of tens and twenties. I've never seen this much money in my life. I can't stay in here and count it all—the staff might get suspicious. With this much money, I'll never have to worry about paying for the new games, ordering food, or affording my mum's Christmas present ever again.

Leebee offered me more work. I think he's a cool guy. And with this much cash, I'd be stupid to decline.

"Be by the shop, under the tower block, at six. Got it?"

"Got it."

I agreed to Leebee's order as we left the takeaway into the cold night. I couldn't stay too long, I was shivering. It made sense to power walk home. Taking a shortcut involved getting abuse from *The Hillbillies*, but I was prepared for a few dumb insults. As long as I get home quicker. Approaching the house, I slowed down my walk, stuck out my chest, and began to swing my arms. Showing those pricks I'm not afraid because… I'm not.

Here it comes.

I turn to look at *The Three Stooges* sitting in their front-drive, wearing shorts and vests, despite them being so skinny and it's freezing out.

Even though I was prepared to be called '*bum boy*' for the hundredth time, it never came. All three looked away. One went inside the house to hide. Two others bowed their heads, scratching their licey hair, or shuffling awkwardly like Dan does when he's scared.

They're afraid of me.

I've never been so smug or walked as tall. I think I can feel a smirk brewing.

"What's up, man?"

One of them said, quietly, and with a slight tremble.

I wondered if they'd seen me hang around with Leebee and his gang. It must be. It's the only thing that's changed. After years of being bullied by these morons, they're finally giving me some respect. I like it.

Chapter 24

Dan

"You've been looking out that window for some time. You're not, like, going to jump out of it or anything, are you?"

There is nothing in my head that I can say. Despite scratching my chin, disoriented, and frowning to the ground below, I remain thoughtless.

What are Nikki's true intentions? Why has she brought me here? Has her kindness been a ruse? Is this temptress trying to seduce me into a trap?

"Say something. You're scaring me."

Normally, If my quietness does scare someone, then I would feel the need to justify myself. *I'm not a serial killer, honestly.* Currently, it could be an excuse to leave.

"I should go. Thank you for fixing my nose and letting me use your facilities to clean myself up. It is appreciated."

"I've scared you haven't I? I guess we won't see each other again?"

"You should not be bothered about the possibility of seeing me again. Do not fret about me. I am no one. Not really."

"You seem like a nice guy."

A big part of me does not feel like I deserve those kind words. Because I don't feel 'nice'. I feel unconcerned about other people.

"I try to be nice."

"I also think you're quite cute."

Nikki pulls a flirty mischievous grin.

"Still, you need to work on your hair, and all your teenage, hormonal acne vibe, that's going on there."

"Charming."

"It's not all bad. You have nice long legs. And you are the complete opposite to all the boys I usually date. Believe me—I can sure pick them."

You are pregnant with a crime boss's grandchild.

Of course, I never said that out loud.

"I don't know what it is about bad boys. They get me so wet. I can't help myself. You know the type I mean—moody men, who need therapy."

Wait. Does she know I'm regularly seeing the school psychologist weekly?

"All that has to change, now I have a baby."

"Does Victor Romeo want his grandchild?"

"He does."

Nikki caresses her unborn child gently.

"I need to find a way to get my baby boy away from him. I don't want him growing up to be like Joel."

A cruel, remorseless murderer?

"How are you going to do it? How are you going to protect him, if you can't leave town?"

"The best way is to live with my cousin, in Australia. We keep in touch by *Messenger*."

"What if he finds you in Australia?"

"He'll be at war with the Australian Mafia, The Honoured Society if he steps foot in their turf."

"Why?"

"It's complicated. And Joel didn't tell me everything about the business."

"What is stopping you?"

Nikki burst out in a humourless laugh.

"With what cash? I have no passport. I can't afford a flight. I'd have to pay for my mum, and my little bambino."

I wish I could help her, but this is completely out of my hands. Also, I have my own plans to sort out. I need to get to Hampshire. If I hadn't made a promise to Joe, then maybe I could have taken Nikki and the child, instead.

Hang on their cowboy. You have just met this girl. How are you going to raise a child? You can barely take care of yourself. How can you tend to a baby?

You will not be a good parent. "The apple doesn't fall far from the tree." Your parenting skills will only be as good as your own. Despite their problems, they are better off without you.

"At least let me give you some of Joel's hair wax he left. It's not like he's going to be using it anytime soon."

The subject is dropped, thankfully.

Nikki holds her bump, as she sits herself up. She takes a few steady breaths, in preparation to stand, but I halt her progress.

"I don't want anything from him," I declined.

Nikki seemed surprised that I declined free luxuries, but, morally, she understood.

"Well, take my advice and buy some hair gel and cream of your own."

"I have no money."

That was shameful to say. Women prefer strong guys who protect them. Successful men, with their own house and lots of money. I am neither of those things. Strong women like Nikki shall not be falling head-over-heels for a loser—like me—anytime soon.

"Steal them, don't pay for them."

There was something troublesome in her smile, and those eyes something alluring—dangerous. Many men would have been seduced into her bidding.

"That will be wrong."

"I guess you'll remain a virgin forever."

"How did you know I was a virgin?"

"I do now. I bet you've never even kissed a girl."

My heart leapt into my throat, leaving it dry. I can feel my pale complexion turning red.

"Sit down. I'll show you how to do it."

I returned to the makeup chair, sitting opposite Nikki.

She places both her delicate hands on my thighs. Then starting to gently caress them forwards. Her nails draw nearer, and nearer, to my crotch. The touch of her smooth palms on my hard thighs, caused the little hairs on my neck to raise up. She tilts her head and lures her cherry red lips nearer to me. I'm so nervous, I could just crumble in front of her. I feel the sweat forming on my brow.

My hands! What do I do with my hands?

Unsure where to place my hands. Unsure if I have permission to hold her body tightly. I just placed them on the soft duvet.

I can smell the cigarette smoke from her breath. Then our lips briefly connected. Nikki pulled back. giggles. Then gripped my trim hips firmly. I can feel her nails digging into my bones. The rush of blood would cause me to bleed out more. But I don't mind. I would happily bleed for her.

Nikki leaned forward again.

Wanting to be more decisive, I took control over my nerves by dominating her body. I dug my fingertips into her back, pulling her up. I am going to take charge. Be more decisive. I want to stand up and be closer to her. So that's what we're going to do.

Her legs began to wobble. She found balance by placing her hands on my chest.

Simultaneously, we both closed our eyes, as the kissers welcomed each other in. The heat from our bodies was so unbearable, we ripped each other's clothes off.

She leant on her bed seductively. Biting her lip. Placing her hands over her head, gripping onto the rails, submissively.

On the bed, I fell to my knees. Moved my head in between her inviting legs. My hands brushed against her soft pale thighs. I gripped the lace of her black lingerie. Slowly removing them from their owner.

I leant forward over Nikki, being mindful of her stomach. Tasting those red lips again, and again. Sloppier than I wanted. Yet, there was a raw, primitive, and passionate hunger inside, one that just wanted more—and more. I kissed the side of her neck, shoulders, and all around her upper body.

My hips gently swayed to and from her.

Am I doing this right? What if she's not enjoying this?

All the questions spun around my mind. Until—

Nikki started to groan in my ear, her breathing was shorter and quicker. Giving me some reassurance. And confidence. My body was more vigorous. Her moaning was louder.

I didn't want this to end…

… But I soon had to pull out.

Discomfort. Regret. Embarrassment. Anger. These were among the emotions, which rained down on me, like a ton of bricks. I hung from the edge of the bed in shame.

Nikki laughed at me. She put her arm on me, reeling me back into bed.

"I'm sorry." I couldn't apologise enough.

"Don't be daft. It was your first time."

"How was it?"

Don't ask that!

"It was… alright."

The long pause before 'alright' was deeply unsettling.

"It was nice."

She smiled.

"I thought it was only meant to be a kiss."

We both laughed.

Nikki's hands rubbed my chest, and I wrapped my arm around her sweaty body. We lay together in silence. I have never been in such a state of tranquillity. I could just lay in her arms, here, forever.

Chapter 25

Joe

A black *Ford* car rolls up in front of the shop. It stops pretty much in front of me. There's something unnerving about this. I can't see through the tinted windows.

Who's in the car?

The window slowly lowers.

A guy who's masking his face with a bandana peeps out…

"Where you from?"

I didn't answer.

We continue dead-eying each other.

He points apiece out the window. The man shoots me in the middle of the street. My body rapidly jolts as it's pierced with bullets. It all happens so quick I don't feel anything. Not until I hit the concrete, where I bleed to death slowly. I cry out in pain. But no one around me cares enough to help, they just walk by as if they were expecting me to get shot.

That's what I imagined. I was relieved when I saw Leebee.

The car journey was quiet. All I kept thinking was how stupid I was being. Jumping to a paranoid delusion like that. As if some randomer would draw a gun and shoot me for no reason.

It won't be for reason, Joe. You're in a gang now.

It could happen anytime, in a gang or not. Someone might mistake me for someone else. Someone might just want to hurt someone for no reason. Protection from Leebee, and the boys, will keep me safer.

"Where are we going?"

I had to ask.

Leebee sits in the passenger seat. I look at the driver, then towards the dude next to me (Darnell). As if they're exchanging some secret message. Then Leebee turned towards me.

"We got a meet, wi'd the boss."

I was puzzled, I thought Leebee was the boss. Then it hit me. I had forgotten we were all working for Victor Romeo.

Being in the presence of a top gangster was scary. He had two well-built bodyguards, reputation, power, REAL power. He looks just like the billboards for his estate agents. Dark afro, well-trimmed goatee. Fully suited and booted. Expensive black leather gloves, with matching shoes. He's staring at Leebee, who's sat next to him on a park bench, sipping his coffee cup with such a calm posture. Even though he had a handsome smile and a certain coolness to him. Behind those dark eyes you know he's plotting something, calculating something, something evil. It was making Leebee nervous. I have never seen him look so worried. And If he's worried then I definitely am. It's probably a good thing I'm standing by the car, with the driver and Darnell. I tried to eavesdrop, but I struggled to catch everything that's been said.

"Hello. Mr Romeo."

"Leebee. How is the movement of my new product?"

Victor spoke quietly, smoothly, and even sounded educated. But there was still a certain roughness in his tone. No matter how hard you leave your roots, you still can't fully polish them away. You can leave and go to a bigger house. Meet smarter friends. Dine in the fanciest of restaurants. That little niggle. Such as a rough tone. It's there to remind you—at the end of the day you are, and always will be, from a shithole like Desby.

"It's good. Mr Romeo. Like you said. We're selling *Spice* for what? A tenner or so more than cocaine. And it's cheaper to make."

"Good. Just as long as the money keeps coming in."

He licked his lips when he said money. I guess that's the *ting* he likes the most. Not his son. Maybe if he wasn't such a terrible dad, Joel wouldn't have stabbed Michael Clark. I can feel my nails dig into my hands, as I form a fist.

"What about the problem?"

"I have a plan…"

Wait. There's a problem? Is it me? Is it why I'm here?

They continue talking, but I can't hear anything.

"Is there anyone that can step up?" Victor asked.

"There might be."

Leebee turns to look at me.

Victor Romeo follows his direction. He begins to study, investigating me.

"I tink he be loyal."

"Ah. Ah. Ah. It is pronounced: 'I think he will be loyal'. You're not going to use any street talk within my presence."

"Yes—yes. I'm so sorry, Mr Romeo."

"What about…?" I wish Darnell and the driver would stop talking, so I can hear.

Victor glanced at his flashy Rolex.

"That will be all for now. I'll arrange another appointment in about four months. Till then, you know how to contact me if there's an issue."

"Yes, sir."

"Good."

Leebee returned to the vehicle, looking relieved that the meeting was over.

"We got work to do."

We all hopped in the vehicle.

"What is *Spice*?"

Darnell laughed at my stupid question.

Leebee peered in the rear-view mirror to talk to me.

"It's like weed but four times as strong. It's barely legal shit. Don't ever smoke it, actually when you're rolling with us. You won't be takin' any*'ting*. You gotta be wi' it, at all times. Feel me?"

I nodded to agree.

Going back, I remember seeing that guy passed out on the main street. I wonder if he had been smoking that shit? If I were to guess, I'd say so. The ting that troubled me the most was wondering what those 'problems' were. And what does it have to do with me?

Chapter 26

Dan

The second the school bell rang. I went straight to Nikki's. Going to hers has been the highlight of the day, no week. Month? Perhaps, a lifetime? Being around her has caused a light to over illuminate the empty gloaming dullness inside. Making me realise, for many years, I have been a numb shell working on auto-pilot. An empty zombie, passing the time through routine. Wake up in the morning—spend an hour deciding if I should get out of bed. Then, go to school, meet Joe, or run, or go to the library to avoid The Mother. Then—go to bed with the headphones in. Now, there is a fresh course of electricity running in my veins. A burning flame of excitement, caused by the visits to my girlfriend's.

Do you think that's a bit too soon, Dan? You still don't know much about her. She had intercourse with you on the first date. Can you assume Nikki does that with lots of other people?

The past is lustreless. The only thing tangible in the future, and the choices we make to further develop the time ahead.

Is choosing to care for a murderer's son a good choice for the future?

Am I the only person who has a war inside their head? I assure myself by realising, our relationship is currently in very early stages. Momentarily, there is no need to commit to a monumental lifestyle change.

I soon ended up at the bike sheds. One of those moments where you were so in deep thought, you are completely surprised by your whereabouts. Behind the young eleven-year-old smokers stood a familiar face, with a spiked Mohican haircut. Wearing a cut-out denim jacket, which was covered in sewn-on patches of band names and their logos. There was no chance in hell—anyone can read the band names of those patches. It was Sam, kneeling on the ground, rolling up a joint.

"You're not going to rat on me, are you?"

He should have performed the deed in an inconspicuous area if he was really that concerned. Of course, I was not going to tell the teacher. 'Snitches get stitches' and all that.

"Cause, you look like a stiff."

"Don't worry."

Sam bursts into laughter.

"I'm only joking, man."

"I like the patches on your denim jacket. Most of the time I'm wearing a band shirt out of school."

"Knock-offs, or from an actual gig?"

"Knock-offs. Unfortunately. I never had the opportunity to attend a concert. I can't afford it."

"*Ahhh.* Man. You have to go to a gig. It's one of the best things ever."

I would have to take his word for it. The sound of being in a room with so many people really wanted me to scratch the walls, or punch someone.

"Right, dude. The other week, I got the bus to London to see *Iron Maiden*. It took me months to save up for. These things aren't cheap, and the prices keep going up every year. All I can say is, it was totally worth it."

"I very much doubt I will have someone to go with."

Hopefully, I did not appear as pathetic as I sounded.

"Go on your own. I did."

That caught me by surprise. I thought everyone was accompanied when attending these events.

"You'll meet people there. On your own, or not. You're at a metal gig. Everyone in that room becomes family. You're all there for one reason, and one reason only. We'll look after each other. if you fall in a mosh pit, some dude will pick you up. If you lose something valuable, 90% of people will hand it in. There's no fighting or hurting each other. Of course, you'll get the odd dickhead, but there're dickheads everywhere."

Sam regained his posture. He placed the spliff behind the ear.

"There're good people out there. You just have to find them. You're not going to do that by not living. If we're not living… then what's the whole point?"

I really liked Sam. He was cool. The point he mentioned echoed through my mind on the way to Nikki's house.

Knocking on her front door, on the crest of her steps I noticed the red *Toyota* was still parked on top of the hill. Not being much of a betting individual, I could quite happily gamble that the vehicle is Big Brother, keeping a watchful eye on her.

"*Hellllo*," the minx said in a flirtatious manner, raising her eyebrows suggestively.

"I told you, you'd look better if you gelled your hair and covered your spots."

I blushed but was delighted when she noticed.

"During lunchtime, Joe had given me some of his wax and face cream."

When she had opened the door, I noticed she placed more white powder on her face. Also, she replaced the red streak with green dye. Going from 'goth' to '*Bride of Frankenstein*'. Of course, I never said that. I am not quite prepared to get my nose broken again.

Inside Nikki's bedroom; we laid on the bed facing each other.

Nikki pulled out her *iPod* and stuck one headphone in my ear. Normally, I would shudder at sharing an earpiece. Not today. I was more interested in her music taste than the fear of sharing germs.

"Who is it?"

"It's *The Offspring*. The song is called '*All I have Left is You*'."

I cringed, expecting the song to be dreary.

"Bands like these: *Blink 182, Sum 41* or *Bowling For Soup*. I used to like it. But we have all matured since then. My music taste has developed with age. Whereas, these bands still act like they are in their teens when they are long in their youth. We all have to grow up at some time."

Nikki rolled her eyes.

"*Jeeez*. You really do take the fun out of everything."

I didn't like how she emphasised 'everything'. It made me sound so sorrowful.

"They still have some good songs. If you could be bothered to sit and listen to them. Then you would know it. So, shut up, open your mind, and give it a listen," she insisted.

Reluctantly, I sampled the music track.

The soft drums were a good start. The delicate vocalist sang about how complicated relationships are. The subdued piano notes were an excellent touch. To help the build-up to the bridge was a subtle guitar being played.

The explosive chorus kicked in, completely blowing my mind away. The masterpiece swayed every cell in my body, causing an internal dance. While my mind was transported into a different place altogether.

"What did you think?"

"I loved it."

Nikki smiled. Which causes me to do the same.

"This is our song now."

I thought that presumptuous, to declare such a bold statement. Although, I had no counterargument.

"So, whenever I'm not here. Or when you leave town to pursue your dreams. This is something to help remember me by. You will listen to this song, and a part of me will be with you for those three minutes."

"I don't know if three minutes will be long enough."

Nikki's face brightened. I expected her to say something mushy in return. Instead, she slapped me in the arm, it was hard enough to bruise.

"You soppy romantic."

Then she laughed in my face.

Earlier, I did tell Nikki my plans about going to a new school in Hampshire. She seemed to be delighted for me. Purposely not mentioning the option to bring a plus one. Not lying. I never want to lie to Nikki. I felt too obliged to take Joe after the promise we made when we were kids.

"Do you have any news on Australia?"

"No. I don't know how I'm going to get there. I don't even know how I'm going to the hospital when I give birth."

"I'll take you."

It's the least I can do.

Nikki squints her suspicious eyes towards me.

"*Youuu.* Can you even drive?"

"My uncle taught me to drive, for a good while, until I lost interest. I will start again."

"Yeah, sure. As long as you don't kill us. Do you even, like, have a car?"

"I'll borrow my uncle's."

Nikki grabs my shirt. Helplessly, I was dragged towards her tense, warm body. Relishing those cherry red lips. All of a sudden, Nikki leapt out of her skin.

"Are you okay?"

Nikki beamed.

"You must be a good kisser. The baby's kicking."

She grabbed my hand and held it on her stomach. I could feel the little foot tapping against my palm. It was... nice. It was... overwhelming. It was... beautiful. My heart melted to the floor. My eyes began to burn. I could not resist the water escaping from my tear ducts. In front of Nikki, I cried. I could feel the drops rolling down my cheek. I had let myself cry next to another human for the first time in nearly a decade. And Nikki didn't seem to mind. She didn't judge. I doubted she'd use it against me. Or thought I was weak. Water arose from her eyes too. These were all tears of joy. This was a new life. This was nothing to be ashamed of. This must be love. I embraced her into my arms, held her very dearly. I could just die, here and now.

"Where is your mother?" I wondered.

"I think she's on a cruise with one of her sugar daddies. I can't remember this one's name."

It sounded like her mother lives a 'colourful' life.

"What you doing over Christmas?" she enquired.

"Christmas is normally an abysmal affair at my house. My mum normally gets drunk and sleeps in."

"Do you want to come over to mine? My mum's away. She says she deserves some more 'me time'. I don't know why. I haven't seen anyone else get as much 'me time' like her."

I contemplate mentioning my mum's battle with alcohol dependence. I decide to keep Nikki completely separate from her. Nikki is not afraid to march over to my house and give my mum atonement. Leaving me to deal with her wrath later. Besides, there's no way I would let my mother near her son.

Nikki remains on the Christmas topic, "I'm not that bothered about Crimbo. The day doesn't live up to the hype. It's just one big disappointment."

I'm not sure. I have a feeling I could enjoy this year's Christmas Day.

"I'm more of a Halloween girl."

"After seeing your horror film collection, I can see why."

She laughed.

"I'm not embarrassed by that. It's not just about the thrill of being frightened. I like the ritual. Trick or treater's."

"I think people wear enough masks."

"I like how in the ninth century our Pagan ancestors would dance in costume, and serve out food, to please the ghosts of the dead that came to haunt us for one night of the year."

"Do you really believe in that superstitious nonsense?"

"I do. It's fun."

"Why's it fun?"

"The mystery. The supernatural. Ghosts. Hidden meanings."

"Such as fortune tellers, or astrology?"

"Yes. I am not stupid. I know there are fakes out there. I also love carving pumpkins."

Pumpkins?

"Pumpkins have several meanings. For example, pumpkin leaves can mean a fresh start—"

"What about a black horse?"

"I thought you didn't believe in this stuff?"

"I had a nightmare once. I can't remember it all, but I recall a pumpkin face, leaves, and a black horse."

"Pumpkin faces can mean you're putting on a face."

I'm starting to believe that possibility.

"What does the black horse mean?"

"The Celts believed the black horse represents the strength of maturity to face whatever life brings. But…"

Nikki paused. Her body became tense, her troubled eyes fixated on me, as she held my hand.

"What is it?" I chuckled.

"The black horse also means death."

Part 3 – As the Seasons Change

Chapter 27

Dan

I gently lift the clutch up, while simultaneously feeding the accelerator. I can feel the old banger vibrate underneath me and Uncle Clive.

His face is disgruntled. I'm sure Uncle C is convinced I'm going to kill him on this icy road. Failing that, the rickety vehicle firing black smog from the rear will spontaneously combust.

"Okay, son. Just take your time."

The car begins to crawl. *Stall.*

In frustration, I hit the car horn. Though it doesn't execute a massive roar. The sound resembles a deflating balloon. Best not press the horn again in case it kills the battery.

"It will take time, but you will get there," he reassured.

"That's the thing. I don't have time."

"Why? Are you planning on robbing a bank, *Dick Dastardly*?"

Uncle Clive bellows at first, till it merges into a squeaky cough. It might be the cold winter air suffocating his lungs.

"Do you want to go to the hospital?"

"No, you cheeky bastard. It's just a damn cough. I'm not dying."

I've noticed he's out of breath more than usual. After a while, Uncle C recuperates. Giving him enough strength to give me a warning.

"I told you, you shouldn't be doing this for one girl. You should be playing the field, while you're young. Not being someone's stepdad at the age of seventeen."

"I like her. She's trouble."

"They always are…" He made a sexist remark, one I wish not to repeat.

"Is this what you really want?"

"I think it is."

Uncle C smiles at me.

"I have never seen you so happy. You smile every time you say her name. What is her name again?"

"Nikki—"

He points his grubby finger at me.

"See. You just did it again. Tell me—did you stick your tackle in her pond?"

My face turns red out of humiliation. I also laugh at the metaphor. Then grinned.

With his muscular arms, he playfully pushes my undersized body against the car window.

"You did, didn't you? You dirty dog."

The fun came to an end when I told Uncle C about the promise I made with Joe. About the gifted school in Hampshire. And how I have been considering taking Nikki and her son with me, instead of Joe.

It took a while for my uncle to gather his thoughts.

"Well. You like this girl. Are you sure she really likes you?"

That really is a good question. I still cannot comprehend someone else liking me for who I really am. It seems so surreal.

"I think so. It's early stages."

"Maybe you should wait a couple of months before you decide."

That's what I did. For now, I'll focus on completing my driving exam. By the end of the weekend, I could drive down the icy road...

By the new year, I could pilot the banger around Uncle C's land.

In the spring, I became competent to drive on my own.

Chapter 28

Joe

I haven't seen Dan in ages. Well, not out of the classroom. I think we both have our own thing now. With his hair done, and most of the acne gone, I wonder if he's seeing someone. I hope he doesn't stuff his pizza down him like he's doing in front of me. That would really put 'em off. Even now, as he's chomping away, a piece of cheese hangs from the corner of his mouth. I know he doesn't care what others think. But I do. It's a good thing I hadn't taken him to *Giovanni's*.

I had taken my side-piece Leah to *Giovanni's*. It was like £20 just for the tomato sauce that goes under the cheese. Leah looked beaut' in her skimpy blue dress, showing those long smooth legs. The lasagne was incredible. Although I didn't really enjoy my meal.

All I noticed were men in suits and their dates—the fake women in long dresses. The type of sluts who dress nice, and smile all the time, but cheat on their partners with younger guys like me. Everyone in that room turned in their seats to measure me up… They whispered things among each other… They were talking about me. They knew… They all knew… I'm a drug dealer. How else could a poor young lad like me afford to eat here? Well, fuck 'em all. I wasn't going to be judged by some fucking snobs. I bet all these people lie, steal, and cheat, in their jobs. The only difference between mine and their jobs is they have names badges and suits. They just looked down at me to make themselves feel taller. I should have gotten used to people looking down at me by now. I deserved respect. The vibration in my pocket brought me back to Dan, and his runner's appetite. I pulled out my mobile. Gemma called me,

What's she want now?

I couldn't be bothered to talk to her. She's been so clingy lately. I declined her call. Thinking I'd text her later on that night, hoping I wouldn't forget again.

If I had taken Dan to *Giovanni's,* he would get suspicious, and start asking questions like *"how did you manage to afford this place?"* I wouldn't have had an answer. All I wanted to do is treat my best friend without being interrogated. Why's that so hard? I can feel myself getting ratty. It's not me, it's these long nights and early mornings for school. It's catching up to me.

Dan stopped eating. He stared at me with a grave expression. Then avoids eye contact. He held his can of *Coke*, rotated it back and forth.

He had some bad news but struggled to find the courage to tell me.

"Joe…"

He sounded so timid.

"I know that we have been friends for a long time. You are, and will always be, my closest friend. I cherish our friendship more than anything."

I can see his eyes going red. *Oh my god…* Is he dying?

"Do you remember the day on the beach? The day we made a blood oath? Well, I do. I had sworn to defend that vow for a very long time."

Where's this going?

"Joe. Do you really want to come with me to the school in Hampshire?"

"Honestly… No. I won't belong there."

There was an awkward silence between us. I knew he wanted to go. I wanted him to go. He deserved a chance to have a good life and have a good job.

Dan used the water to moisten his dry throat.

"Dan. I think you should still go."

I saw that smile, Dan. The one that wasn't hidden well. You were still going to go, with or without me. So, what was the point of asking? You were pretending. You fucking snake.

"There's a tremendous sense of guilt. Leaving without you. Breaking the pack. It is just wrong."

"It's fine."

That's all I could say. I wanted to add *"We'll keep in touch." "You're my boy."* But I never had the heart to say it, so unsure if I'd mean it.

Dan stood up to hug me, I hugged him. But the hug didn't feel like it used to.

"I have to make a move. Thanks again. I would still like to see you over the summer. If that is okay?"

"I don't know. It depends on work."

Dan's face turned even more glum than normal.

"I will see you at graduation. And obviously, we'll celebrate before you go."

He smiled, half-heartedly, and walked out.

Dan had never asked me about my job. He doesn't know I work.

That's because he doesn't care about me anymore. He's already moved on. Maybe it's time I should move on.

Chapter 29

Dan

My early night was disturbed by the banging walls. My mum is hallucinating. I can hear her screaming through the thin walls to my neighbours.

"Get 'em out. Get 'em out. Get 'em out. Get 'em out. Yes. Yes."

She punched walls repeatedly, with it being made out of paper mache, I fear this will cause the house to collapse.

"I know it's you looking at me. I have a *cleeean* house. It's fucking *cleeean*. Are you listening to me?"

Bang *Bang* *Bang*.

"It's you. It's you. You're the dirty fuckers. Stop watching me. I've told you to stop watching me."

The incoherent shrieking continues long into the night. Laying in my bed, all I want to do is curl up into a ball, but I'm too terrified to move a muscle. Now, I can hear her crawling up the stairs, muttering to herself.

What if she comes up into my room? Oh, please don't come into my room. Don't hurt me, mummy. Please don't hurt me. Whatever I did… I'm sorry.

In the room opposite, the beast collapses onto her bed.

In our separate rooms, we eventually fell asleep. Though, it was only me who descended to a dream. Falling. Falling. My body painlessly plummeted vertically onto a tree branch. Due to the dazed state, there was a lengthy amount of time before I could gather my bearings.

It was the forest near Uncle Clive's farm, except in the summertime. There was no sound of birds singing. No warmth from the sun. An unsettling cold silence loomed over the green. There's something that should not be. A dark, ageing log cabin reclines on an empty space surrounded by colourful trees. Tiny white petals trickled down from the overhead branches. The sun seeped through the gaps, illuminating the yellow grass surrounding the cabin. However, the sunlight never shone onto the ancient log home. Making it was worthy of investigation. I stumbled to the open in a drunken stupor. Emerging to the cabin, I noticed there were Anglo-Saxon wyrd symbols carved onto the rough round logs. Stepping inside, the light was dim. Emerging from the sunshine to the dark took time for my eyes to adjust. There were two doors, on either side of me. Ahead of me was a bulky dark ladder.

The ladder of death.

I pace my body to the room on the right. Inside held nothing. A complete absence of light. A vast amount of nothingness. A bottomless pit of emptiness. Oblivion. Should I step into the dark, I would fall into a downward spiral into the darkness. With no hope of return. From the left, is a creaking sound. I cautiously peer into the room to find the source. Inside is my Uncle's old rocking chair, rocking back and forth. Back and forth. The unpleasant creaking swept relentlessly through the room, like grinding teeth. That's enough to make your bones shiver. The swinging must have been caused by a draft. No, not the wind. The motion is caused by the mannequin sitting on the rocking chair. One of those life-size dummies that you can change in any direction. It sits with both hands on the chairs' arms. Its faceless head stares through my soul. I jump out of my skin when I hear, what-sounds-like, a marble hitting the wooden floor. I look towards the open door frame, as I hear it gently rolling down the corridor. The sound grew louder. I expect to see something pass through the open door. Nothing came.

I turn back, to notice the mannequin has moved. It's now pointing and facing a sizable old television. The broken antenna has caused the TV to display nothing but static.

I kneel down in front of the box. The white glare from the TV screen brightens my face along with the inside of my forearms.

A picture appears on the screen. A screenshot of Abbey Road crops up on the TV. It reverts back to static. Then a still image of the A68 in Scotland appears. Static. Khao San Road in Thailand is displayed. Static. A polaroid of my mum. *No, thank you.* Static. Then a picture of Black Mountain Pass in Wales. Static. An image from Route 66. Static.

I get it now. These are images of different roads I could take.

The slideshow of pictures exhibits some lesser-known roads or motorway junctions. Then, there was one picture I was astonished by. It was of Nikki smiling, cradling a new-born baby in her arms. I go to touch it. By the time my fingerprints touch the glass of the screen, it has already changed pictures. Now I'm left holding onto an image of a recently built estate, owned by Victor Romeo. I swipe my hand away to disconnect my fingertips from the TV, leaving smear prints of blood on the screen.

Chapter 30

Joe

Walking home after finishing early on my corner. A black *Ford EcoSport* swerves in front of me. The driver hammered the brakes.

DC steps out of the passenger side of the car. His smile makes my skin want to crawl.

What's he after?

"Bruv. How it be? Get in da car and I'll ge' ya a ride."

An unsettling feeling makes me want to be sick. A terrible gut feeling. Something's not right. DC is never nice to me. His face is trying to look friendly, but his body is so tense.

"No. I don't mind walking, but thanks for the offer."

I go to slide past, but he steps in front of me. Pretending to smile through his yellow teeth.

"What's ya, problem man? All I wanna do is ge ya a ride."

My heart started to beat faster.

"No, but thanks."

DC is not taking 'no' for an answer. He lifted his *Suicide Squad* jumper to warn me with his knife.

"Get in."

His tone went from friendly to threatening.

I froze still. Flashbacks of Michael Clark bleeding on the floor replayed in my head. Is DC going to kill me? He's always hated me. But why? Cause, I'm good looking and he ain't? Maybe it's cause Leebee prefers me over him. He can't kill one of Leebee's soldiers without permission, surely?

The two gorilla-like bouncers stepped out the back doors of the car. They both stand on either side of me. I feel claustrophobic. That's what they want, they want to trap me.

"Get in the back."

It doesn't feel like I had a choice. After climbing into the back of the car, the pair of goons trapped me in the middle. Blocking the doors.

The car drives. I try to view where we're going. It's hard to see with blacked-out windows, and everyone's heads are in the way.

"I'm just left of here."

The driver is quiet. I know he's heard because he's looking at me through the rear-view mirror.

"This left, please."

The car turns right.

I'm gonna die. I'm gonna die. I'm gonna die.

I'm so stiff yet trembling with fear… The heart is pounding. My cheeks are sunk in. I need a piss.

Oh my god. Don't piss yourself, Joe.

I'm too scared to move. Too scared to cry. I just try my best to hold my urine. I think a little bit seeped out as my knee keeps shaking. My eyes are pointing out of my head. I don't know if it's the adrenaline or if I still can't cry.

Not being able to cry is a good thing.

I know—I just don't want to die.

My body feels like it's been wrapped in cling film, I can't breathe.

As the car drives around unfamiliar streets. More and more I'm getting worked up in my head. The more I think, the more I want to piss my pants. I feel warm. No sweat. Not piss. Just really hot on the inside.

They're gonna take me to a ditch and kill me. They're gonna take me to a ditch and kill me. They're gonna—ditch—and kill me. They're gonna kill me.

Now I can feel my wide eyes about to turn red.

The car stops. It's dark. I have no clue where we are.

Now my breathing is uncontrollable. I have images of these men dragging me out the car. Tooth and nail. Stabbing me. Leaving me.

120

At the same time; both men on my side open their doors. DC follows them.

This is it. This is it.

I almost beg... *Please, Please, don't do this. I'll stop. I won't work for you anymore. I'll do anything. Just—just—just don't kill me.*

The door locks. Trapping me inside with the driver.

My heart is thundering, I have so much energy. I can outrun them. When it's the right moment, I'll smash the window and run. Just run. Never look back.

The car boot slams.

I jump out of my skin. I'm such a pussy.

DC leads the muscle as they square up to another gang. One guy has a machete, the other has a baseball bat.

"Pussy hole. What did I tell you about selling on our turf?"

The other gang leader obviously hasn't seen the other boys tooled up. Squares up to DC.

"Back off, bruv."

"Victor Romeo sends a message."

DC stabs the leader repeatedly, blood splashing over his ugly face, and his favourite top. Though DC doesn't mind. He's laughing and howling. Looks like he's enjoying it far too much.

Most of the other crew runoff. While one of our guys swings his baseball bat into another man's face.

The man falls to the floor, wielding his broken face. His puffer jacket does not protect his back from getting pummelled with the baseball bat over and over again.

"You fucking want some. Yeah. Yeah. you fucking want it?" One lad charges to an ape.

King Kong wields the machete, sending it deep into the lads' neck.

The squeal of pain is deafening.

The man who has been hacked wobbles one leg in front of the other, quite comically. With one hand holding the wound, but blood continuously floods out of his neck. His other hand reaches out for balance or help.

My stomach churns, revolted by their actions. I begin to taste a bit of vomit at the back of my throat.

The car's running.

DC and the other guys run back to the *Ford.*

The car pulled away, I noticed the other guy crawling towards us. Either he's going to have some sort of revenge, or we're the closest people that can help him. As if he thought for one second, at the last minute, we'd show remorse, and help him.

In the getaway car. We drove at some speed. Not quite sure to believe what I've just seen. It was like seeing Michael Clark again, but much, much, worse.

"I think they got the message," the driver said jokingly.

Everyone laughed menacingly.

I never found it funny. I can still hear each smack from the baseball bat, it was like wood hitting wood. From those blows, it's bound to leave that guy crippled. That's not all. I still see the other man's face, the face of suffering. Hobbling towards the car, arms reaching out for help. And the blood. So much blood. Gushing out between his neck and shoulder. His cries of pain. I can't shift it out of my head.

The car stops.

DC stops and pulls a sinister grin towards me. After he wipes the blood from his face with his sleeve.

"This is what ya get when ya fuck with us."

I see why DC has brought me now. He wanted to scare me. Well—he's succeeded.

The muscle, *Laurel and Hardy,* step out of the car and begin removing their clothes. It's not a sight I want to see. Though, it's better than DC's icy stare.

"Joe, you've never been one of us. You never will be…"

That hurt. I never wanted DC's approval in the first place. But I felt like I fitted in with Leebee and some of the others.

"Me and Leebee be mates before your bitch ass came along. You gonna be quiet from now on, and I will be lieutenant before you. Feel me?"

I nod.

"You gotta say it."

I gulped to swallow my pride. While he's holding a knife, I don't think I can argue.

"You're going to be lieutenant before me."

"Good."

He slaps my cheek, with his bloody hand. It makes me shriek.

"You don't just work for Leebee anymore. You work for Sticks and me."

I now know that the driver is called Sticks.

"You're gonna ge' us 25% of P's from ya count."

"But that's Romeo's money."

The blade from the knife is inches away from my face.

"Fuckin' argue wid me again, I'll fuckin' cut your throat."

My eyes are stuck on the shank. A slight misstep and it'll get my pretty face cut. I would have to explain it to Dan, my mum, and the girls won't like me anymore.

"I understand."

DC gets the knife out of my face, turns to Sticks.

"Get this pussy-hole to his corner. And den we'll torch the car."

Hate being so small and bullied. I am not being treated with respect like everyone else. With DC around, I'll never be *safe* in the gang. Now, I have to give him some of mine and Leebee's cut. That's ridiculous. Then again, he asked for the cut, *after* Leebee's bouncers stepped out of the car. Maybe, I could use this to my advantage.

That's a risky game, Joe. If Leebee doesn't believe you. DC will kill you.

My inner voice is right. I wonder if anyone else argues with themselves like this? It will have to be a last resort.

Maybe Leebee is right. You're not one of them. Maybe, it's time to get out while you can.

That voice of reasoning is right. I think I'll take Dan on his offer, It'll be safer at this posh school. It'll be safer in Hampshire.

Chapter 31

Dan

After my morning session with my counsellor, Gareth, I was pleased to hear the student accommodation at school in Hampshire can accommodate myself, Nikki, and a child. Providing, I get my expected grades. Pretty certain, I will achieve it. The exams were effortless. Only one left to go. Things are in motion…

How do you think Joe did on his examinations?

I turn from my usual seat, to view Joe. He looks petrified. I don't know what happened, but the brown from his skin has disappeared. He is also using the surface of the desk to mask his shaking hand.

Something bad is going to happen, Dan. Nothing good will ever come your way.

If I really do desire to murder something, then I wish it slaughters the negative part of me. I have not had any visions since my continued weekly sessions with the psychiatrist.

Are you happy to explain your dream last night? What did that all mean? Blood? Ladder of death? The symbols about destiny?

Shut up. Shut up. Shut up.

The only good thing about your dream was you chose not to descend into the dark oblivion.

I can no longer revert to the depressing empty shell. I have a purpose now—protecting Nikki and her son from Victor Romeo.

Who's going to protect them from you?

The Headmaster enters Mr Ford's class, then directly addresses me.

"Mr Suddlemire. You need to go to the hospital. Right away."

I ran to the hospital as fast as I could. My school shoes are pummelling the ground, and sure to be ruined by the end of it. Shoving past strangers who are passing by as I sprint down the roads. Normally, I wouldn't do such a thing, but my mind was elsewhere. Why did I not pass my driving test sooner? Is it the baby? Is the little boy alright? Is Nikki alright? Who's holding her hand?

The white shirt is now damp with sweat. I regained my breath, but my aching legs could barely walk. To make things worse, the visitor's lift is broken. So, I had to stumble up the stairs to the maternity ward. Which was on the top floor. The level below must have been where the operating theatre is held. One nurse walked out, dressed in full PPE: apron, gloves, hairnet, shoe covers, visors, and mask. It was an interesting look.

Eventually, I climbed up to the fifth floor. My body fought off the strong compulsion to collapse on a visitors chair. I want to see Nikki, and our baby.

Did I just say 'our' baby?

But, there's an issue. Guarding the door was Victor Romeo holding a bouquet of flowers. By the side of the crime boss were two hired, military-grade bodyguards. They looked the part with their suits, earpieces and still wearing sunglasses, despite being indoors.

Victor Romeo turned around, he smiled at me as if he knew who I was.

"Hello. Young man. Who are you here to see?"

He asked me in a patronising tone.

His presence was intimidating. I never replied.

"I can see that you have run here. Don't worry, boy. Nikki and the baby are alright."

Keeping quiet, I debated how he knew me. It came to me. The red *Toyota* parked on the street. It must have followed us around from her house to the shops, to the free birthing classes at the community hall.

"What's your name son?"

"Dom," I lied.

"Dom. I would like to thank you for everything that you have done." Victor gave the purple flowers to one of his goons.

Opening his leather wallet, he pulled a bundle of money from it. Proceeded to flicker through the individual notes. Almost like the mob boss was flaunting his rich status. He then offers me a heap of cash.

"Thanks for the offer, but I was just happy to help."

"Are you sure? It's the least I can do. Take it. You've earned it."

Victor winks at me, before representing a charming white smile.

"Really. I like Nikki. I was happy to help."

Victor seemed to be impressed. He sticks his pay-off back in his wallet. Shoves it back in the inside pocket of his extravagant suit.

"Dom. Thank you for your help. But this is a *family matter* now."

In other words—you're no longer welcome to stay.

I leave the hospital, regretting my cowardice. Beating myself as I wish there was more that could have been done. But who am I? I'm no one. I can't take on Victor Romeo. Especially on my own. If the police can't—I have no chance.

Outside, the sun is scorching, but a light breeze cools me down. I browse each and every one of the hospital's windows. Dreaming that Nikki is eying me through one of them. But that's what our life together is… a dream.

Chapter 32

Joe

I travelled to the beach by train. I got rid of my bike. It felt foolish keeping such childish things.

Gazing over the black rails, I watched families playing in the sand. Smelling fresh fish 'n' chips. The doughnut vendors. Arcades. The sound of seagulls flocking in the air. These things all remind me of the times me and Dan came here.

We had so many happy memories at this place. Playing in the sand. Swimming in the chilling sea where the tide would drag you out in a matter of seconds. Checking out the girls. Finding pennies on the floor to go to the arcade machines. Imagining that we live in those flats facing the pier.

Those things don't mean anything to me now. I can see what Dan said when he said, "*we can no longer hide from the big—bad—world. We can no longer avoid reality by reading, playing Xbox, going on our log swing on the track, spending the school holidays in our den in the woods, or cycling our way out of this town to get away. What happened to Michael Clark has really burst the bubble.*"

The adult world is a sharp pin. No. Not a pin. A knife. One that has not just burst our bubble. It has killed our innocence.

Dan finally arrived. He locked his bike up against the hot handrails.

"Hello, Joe. Why are we meeting here? Why the urgency?"

His face is super depressed. But Dan always looks like that. I have bigger problems. My life is at stake.

"I had to come here because it's safer."

He's confused.

"What do you mean, Joe?"

… I told him everything. From joining Leebee's gang to DC threatening to kill me, like he murdered the boys from the other gang.

Dan paced up and down. Pressing fingertips so hard into his eyes, they could have popped.

"Fuck."

He yelled in his hands until his little face went red.

"Why did you do something so stupid? What were you thinking?"

"I was thinking I didn't have a choice. I had no prospects. No brains to get into a college. The money was great. I made some new friends."

"Your so-called friends are drug dealers, Joe. They will not have your back."

"They've had my back more than you've done."

"What does that mean?"

"If shit goes down. They wouldn't run off and leave me."

"I would never leave you. But you must be smart and learn to pick your fights."

"Well, I'm cornered now. I need your help, Dan."

Dan's face was worried, but his help didn't look promising.

"I need you to take me to the posh school in Hampshire. Get me away from here."

Dan shakes his head.

"Dan. We made a promise. Right here. On this very beach. A blood pact. We're blood brothers."

Dan's eyes started to cry. It irritated me.

"Stop crying. Man up."

There's no room for weakness in this world.

"I can't take you. I am already taking someone else now."

"Who?"

"Nikki Yakes."

I laughed in his face.

"You must be kidding."

"I'm not joking. I told you this, the last time I saw you. The time when you bought me pizza."

I am quite forgetful, but there was no way he mentioned Nikki Yakes in the *Pizza Shop*.

"You're lying. You never told me anything about her."

"I'm not lying."

"You always lie."

"Says you. When were you planning on telling me that you are a drug dealer?"

"I know what you're doing. You're making me think that I've forgotten about Nikki Yakes. When the truth is, you were too chicken shit to tell me."

"I think you're getting paranoid."

I can't get my head around all this,

"I can't believe you're taking that slut—"

"Don't call her that."

"Dude, you can't pick her over me. 'Bro's before hoe's', and all that."

"Nikki is a good person, who wants a better life for her son. She is in some troubled water. I want to help her."

"Even, *I* know that baby is Joel Romeo's. It was in trouble before it was born. It'll grow up to be a murdering bastard like its dad. That's who we become—our dads."

"Are you saying we'll be like our dads? Dead or gone?"

Dan crossed the line. The urge to punch him was unreal. This time I won't care if I break his nose.

"You do realise I'm going to get killed. I'm your best friend."

"What happened to 'I am my own man'? That's been your attitude for the last few months."

"So, this is it? This is the thanks I get for all the years I've helped you. You're gonna ditch me for some bitch."

Dan pushed me, though I don't wobble far. I was surprised by Dan's aggression.

"Do not refer to Nikki in that way."

The skinny boy trying to threaten me was amusing. How about this for size?

"If you do not take me to this posh school. I will tell Victor Romeo about your plan to hide Nikki and his grandson from him."

Dan looked petrified now.

"You wouldn't."

Calling my bluff might be a mistake.

"I guess you'll have to find out."

"I'll report you to the police. You'll be arrested, and your mum will be devastated. Crushed to discover her only son is some degenerate lowlife."

I punch Dan hard in the ribs. The cracking sound was music to my ears.

Dan's puny body could not handle the blow. He lays on the ground, coughing, and gasping for air.

"If you ever mention my mum again I'll kill you."

I stand over him. Proving myself to be the dominant one of the two, just as I've always been.

"You idiot. Do you know anything about the street? You rat on us, *den* you and Nikki will definitely be dead."

Dan used the rails to pull his weak body up. I watched as he struggled. He used an arm to cradle the damaged rib.

"I have no understanding of the culture…"

Dan breathing was still heavy. He glared at me with such hatred in his eyes.

"Neither do you. It's not like it will matter—you cannot commit yourself to anything. You will do something for a while. Pretend to know everything about that subject. Then you get bored and leave."

There's something truthful in this. Like boxing, taekwondo, or relationships. I'm really excited about it, at first, till I drop out. That's what makes me mad the most. I storm off, heading back to the train station. Sitting on the old shaky seat, which may have chewing gum stuck underneath. My head vibrates on the single glazed window. Watching the farmers' fields fly by. I considered what Dan said. Guilt smacks my face like the windowpane does when we travel over a slight bump. I may hate his fucking face, but he must know—I'll never tell his plan to Victor Romeo. Another ting. It might be hard now, but I'm gonna stop being a quitter. I ain't gonna let DC bully me out of the crew. I'm gonna stick out my job to the very end.

Besides, I know the reason why DC hasn't killed me yet. There is still one other problem. A problem where Leebee and Romeo have a plan for me. That's something I can take advantage of.

Chapter 33

Dan

We're finished. Done. Our friendship has ceased. I can't even recognise Joe anymore. He is nothing but a thorn in my side. Literally speaking. It feels like my right rib has been stabbed. I can barely breathe and my temperature is spiking.

It's so hot.

The walk from the beach isn't as long as I remember. Probably because my legs are longer, and I'm not as fat. Being in so much pain, the trek felt like an eternity. I needed to rest. I contemplated dropping my bike along the way so I wouldn't put all my weight to one side or stretch the rib that's broken. I made it to Nikki's. I hope she lets me in.

Will she ever forgive me for not being at the birth?

The pain may give me some sympathy points.

Nikki wasn't the same. She was... quiet. This is unusual for her. Normally, she can't stop jabbering. The only time she remained silent was in her sleep. With no black eyeshadow and white face powder, I can see the bags under her sad eyes. I wish that I could summon up some words of comfort. Instead, I just stare at her while she's sulking under the bed covers.

"I'm sorry, for being so quiet. The baby didn't sleep last night."

She spoke first. Which was a relief.

"It's okay. How is he?"

"He's fine. Thanks."

The baby slept beside Nikki's bed. I leaned over the cot. There, a beautiful baby boy lays, safely wrapped inside a blue blanket, with a matching little blue hat to protect his tiny ears.

"What's his name?"

"Alfie."

She stares at me vacantly.

"I'm sorry I wasn't there. I ran all the way from school—"

"Don't bother. I know why you weren't there…"

Because I'm a coward. Who should have defied Victor Romeo and been there with you? Holding your hand.

"Because I'm a mess."

I wasn't expecting her to say that.

"You don't want to be with a hot mess like me. I'm not even 'hot' anymore. With my baby fat and stretch marks. I'm just a mess. One big fucking slag. Stupid enough to get pregnant by some fuck-boy. You weren't at the birth…"

Her eyes streamed with tears.

"You wasn't at the birth because you realised you were too good for me."

I leapt to her side. Place a hand on her shoulder. Stared into her red eyes.

"Nikki, you are a wonderful person. You took me in when no one else would."

She buried her head into her hands. Though, I refuse to let her believe she doesn't deserve to be loved. I shake her shoulders some more until her eyes meet mine again.

"Look at me. You don't know how much I believe you're the one who's too good for me. You don't know how much I've treasured our time together. You don't know how much you mean to me."

We hug each other. I embrace her warm body. I feel her soft black hair on the side of my cheek. Then the pain in my rib started to flare. I sat down, wielding my pain. I never thought breathing could hurt so much. Nikki nursed me, again.

"What happened?"

"I had a fight with Joe."

"What about?"

"I told him that I was taking you with me, away from here."

A mixture of surprise and confusion was written on her face.

"What are you on about?"

"I got offered a place in a new school, one for the gifted. It's in Hampshire."

"I don't even know where Hampshire is."

132

"It's further away from here."

"They're not going to take me and Alfie."

"Yes, they are. Arrangements have been made. Our accommodation is sorted."

Nikki is still perplexed.

"Victor will kill us both for Alfie. Are you really willing to risk your life for us?"

"Being with you is the only time I really feel… *alive*."

"How could we pull it off? He'll find us."

"Not if we don't tell anyone."

"There's literally a car outside the doorstep. How can we sneak past him?"

"We need to create a distraction. Something grand. So immense that it will distract Victor Romeo and his crew."

"Like what?"

"What if the police arrest the whole gang?"

"It won't work Dan. Some of the police are in Victor's pocket. He has the best lawyers, and Leebee and the boys know, if they talk, they'll get shanked."

"Someone will talk. Someone who doesn't belong there. Someone young. Someone who will be petrified of prison. Someone who's in over his head."

"He'll get killed."

"He might go into witness protection."

"You can't say that for sure."

"It's a risk I'm willing to take… for us."

Chapter 34

Joe

Sitting next to Sticks was more than uncomfortable. The silence made it worse. The sun from his new *Range Rover's* windows made the car sweltering. My blue top was getting damp. I couldn't take anymore, there were too many burning questions inside my head, and the stillness had to be broken.

"Why am I here? Are you here to take more of Leebee's and my money?"

"Shut up, man," Sticks harshly replied.

He stuck out his hands. I noticed that there was a scar across his palm.

"Give me your P's."

I assumed 'P's' meant pounds or pence. Reluctantly, I grabbed my wallet and gave all the sheets I'd earned. That was my money. I worked it for it. It belonged to me. Seeing Mr *Crazy Taxi* licking his thumb to count *my* money. Made me want to go home and put it all in a washing machine to clean it. He pocketed half and gave the half back to me. I wanted to punch him hard in the face. Tell him to give me it back, or I'll run him over with his own wheels. But I'll know he'll kill me or get his psycho-of-a-mate DC to do the dirty work.

"It's wrong, you know. You and DC, taking money that belongs to me and Leebee."

"Bruv…"

I ain't your fucking, bruv.

"All new recruits gotta do it. One day, you'd be taken' P's from young soldiers."

"No, I won't. I'll take home, my share, and my share alone."

He laughed.

"Why are we sitting here?"

"See, that boy, over *der*."

I did. It was the young soldier, short hair and blue chequered shirt. He looks familiar. Leebee pointed him out earlier, as the young lad who was beaten by his step-dad. The one who the boys "sorted out".

"What about him?" I asked.

"The boy be holding out on us."

"He's stealing from us."

"Ye, we gotta put a stop to it."

"Did Leebee tell you to do this?"

"Stop askin' questions, bruv."

Sticks lean over and puts his hand underneath the seat. He grabs what appears to be… a gun.

A chill runs up my spine. I had never seen a gun before.

"Wait. He's just a kid."

I grabbed Stick's arm. He stared back at me with his empty eyes.

"He's a problem, it's gotta be done."

I stare out at a young, skinny, boy, in a blue chequered shirt. Laughing and joking with his mates. So full of life. So many promises. I bet he hasn't even kissed a girl yet. I think back to Michael Clark. He was so young as well.

"It doesn't have to be like this," I insisted.

"It does. Now get off my arm."

"We'll talk to him. Scare him. He's young, so he still has time to learn."

"What if he don't learn?"

"Then we'll do it your way."

Sticks appeared to be convinced. He dropped the piece in his hand. I heard it thud against the floor. It was a relief.

"But you have gotta do it," he demanded.

"Okay."

I walked over to the boy. Sticks tagged along.

The boy in the blue shirt spotted us. His bright white smile turned to a glum and timid head bow. He dawdled towards us, fiddling with his hands.

"We just want to have a word with you. That's all."

I smiled, in an attempt to make the boy believe that he can trust me.

Of course, he's not going to trust you, Joe.

135

He looked over my shoulder. Seeing Stick's more hardened, and spiteful face only made him shake.

"Where are we going?" he spoke so quietly.

"Just someplace quiet, then we'll drop you off back here, with your friends."

Even his pals looked petrified.

"Okay," he agreed hesitantly.

I placed a hand on his back, as I and Sticks walked him over to the *Range Rover*.

The boy kept his head down the entire journey. When the car stopped I could see the terror written all over his body. I had been sitting where he's sat now. I know the horrific thoughts that are going around in his head. All you can think is... *you're going to die.*

Sticks opened up the car door and pulled the boy out from the car by his skinny, frail arm.

Then he pulled the boy to a quiet alleyway. The kid never resisted, but you could tell he didn't want to be here.

"Go on. Joe. Do it."

The boy's eyes widened with fear. He pouted his chest like he was wheezing like he was having an asthma attack. He jumped to the back of the wall, his arms spread out against the brick wall. I felt sorry for him. He's already had years of his stepdad's abuse. He doesn't need any more. I wish Sticks wasn't here, then I could have had a quiet word with the lad instead of having to hurt him.

"Have you been stealing from us?"

He shakes his head.

"Speak up!" I screamed.

"N-no-no."

I looked down his vibrating legs and spotted a pair of brand new red trainers.

"Where did you get your fresh creps?"

He kept quiet.

I punched him in his tiny face. He tumbled down to the ground. To keep him down, I rested my knee on his spine. With one hand I pressed his face against the concrete, the other I twisted his arm around the back.

"You're lying to me. Aren't you?"

"Yes. Yes. I took some money, I'm sorry."

It is almost comical with his cheeks squished together.

"Are you going to do it again?"

"No, No, mister. I promise. I promise."

"How much did you take?"

His body squirmed underneath mine, trying to fight me off, but he wasn't going anywhere anytime soon.

"Two hundred."

"How much?"

I twisted his arm around even further. He squealed in pain.

"Two hundred. Two hundred."

"Are you sure?"

"Yes. Yes. Nothing more. I swear."

"Are you going to pay it back?"

"Yes. Yes. I'll do anything. Please. You're hurting me."

"Good. We want it back with interest. You have one month to work it off."

"Okay. Okay. I'll do it. I promise. Please get off me."

"You best get back to work then."

I twisted his arm even further. Guilt hit me like a car when I broke his arm.

Sitting back in the *Range Rover*. I gazed out the window. Hating myself. I didn't feel bigger or better by bullying a twelve-year-old boy. *At least he'll still be alive...* That's what I told myself to help me ease my conscience.

"We best get *dat* money back otherwise you'd be a dead man too, bruv."

Hearing Stick's voice made me realise something.

"So it's alright for you and DC to steal but not that boy?"

"*Der's* a difference, bruv. Leebee doesn't know anythin' 'bout mine and DC's shit."

After all the commotion with the young soldier, I realised that I forgot to turn off the recorder on my phone.

Chapter 35

Dan

My exams came to an end. They were as easy as the OCR could make them. Now, the hot sun spreads as long as the day. I did not attend my prom; it felt like a meaningless ceremony. Besides, who would have accompanied me?

With school finished, I had six weeks to myself. The past five weeks have been productive. I searched Desby for Joe and his crew. Drug dealers aren't that difficult to detect. They are not the most inconspicuous folk.

It was surprisingly easy to survey how they work. Studying their patterns. Learning how they operate. It was all quite an ingenious scheme. On the edges of the town, by the high rises, someone in a green puffer jacket was selling their substances near the basketball court.

There were kids playing on that court, scumbag.

Also, they owned two separate flats. Each in separate buildings. Only one was operating at a time. Mondays, Tuesdays, Thursdays, and Saturdays, drug users would go to the East Block. On the remaining days, the addicts would have to go to the West Block to purchase their fix.

In the centre of town, a beefy man with a duffle bag would walk up and down the high street between six and seven, nine and ten, twelve and one, three and four, six and seven, half eight till half nine, and finally eleven and midnight. The following day, a ragged girl with dreadlocks would operate the High Street.

The beach had a very similar pattern, Someone would stand outside the arcades. Not *Coin Slots* because that one actually belonged to Victor Romeo. I safely assumed that he didn't want his establishments to be associated with any of his own supplies. I studied the patterns whilst disguising myself as a one-pence machine enthusiast, or while sunbathing on the beach.

For a week, a young-looking man would stand there in a green cap between ten and one, three and five, and six and eight. The following week he would stand in a different location throughout 7:00 a.m. to 9:00, 11:00 to 1:00 and 4:00 and 7:00. Finally, 8:15 till 9:00.

They must lose a lot of money, not being in on a twenty-four-hour service in the main populated areas. However, it does reduce the risk of being caught. I doubted they're afraid of the competition. Or should I say, is the competition afraid of them? Before the summer began, I read an article about a rival drug gang that was attacked.

One was hacked to death by a machete, and one unfortunately survived. He's now permanently crippled due to spinal injuries. It kills me inside, to think Joe is associating with these thugs. I might not know him as well, but at least I know he's not capable of murder.

On the fifth week of my school holiday, I decided to bring my investigation to the vicious streets of boarded-up houses, with their weeds seeping through patio floors and their congregation of the lowlifes. I started at the place where Leebee asked Joe to find him. A year ago when me and Joe were walking home, Leebee's car pulled up, asking if we knew Nikki Yakes? Before they left, Leebee said, *"O'right Joe, if you wanna get some work? Find me on Archers Road."*

Archers Road... That's where Joe could be.

I heard the dealers were no longer exchanging supplies on that road for a while. That must have changed because they were operating again. Whilst writing my notes in the notepad, I had felt a gaze upon my back. I turned around to see if my cover had been discerned. Joe's eyes were fixed on me.

Chapter 36
Joe

"We've got a grass."

Leebee spread the news in the *Range Rover*. His manner was very suspicious. His dark eyes studied me, Darnell and DC from the rear-view mirror. Probably, to see how we reacted. I didn't move. The news hadn't sunk in just yet.

"What?" I repeated.

"Someone has told the police about our man on the pier. He's been arrested on possession."

"Do you think it was one of us?"

My question got more of a longer suspicious stare from our boss. The gaze lasted a long time, creating an uncomfortable silence during the ride.

Have I made myself a suspect? He must know it wasn't me. I don't know who the man on the pier is. Best keep quiet. If I come across too defensive. I'll be more of a suspect.

"We don't know who it was. Victor has asked me to organise an emergency meeting. An example must be made."

I wasn't what he had meant, but I wondered where Sticks was driving us to. We approached the 'You're now leaving Desby' sign. Sticks placed on the headlights on full beam to light up the darkened narrow country lanes.

We're driving to the middle of fucking nowhere in the dead of night… "an example must be made." This isn't going to be good.

Darnell wrapped his rain jacket around him. While he was zipping up, I noticed his hands were shaking. Darnell observed the darkness, hoping we wouldn't see his worry. If fear had given a scent off, as an aftershave would, Darnell would be wreaked in the stuff.

Darnell wouldn't have told the Feds. He's such a cool dude. We've spent many hours on Call of Duty together. I love his passion for break dancin'. The guy has got some serious moves.

Then I couldn't help but question myself.
DC, however, was the opposite. He kept as cool as ice.

It wouldn't be DC, he's Leebee's arse-licker. He might be a psycho, but he's so ambitious—so determined to be a lieutenant.

DC had bought a new *Primark* hoodie. It had *Superman's S* symbol. It was quite ironic because no one saw him as a superhero.
The ground beneath had begun to be rocky. We must have been driving on a farmer's muddy field. It's too dark outside to tell.

There's another person who could be involved. Someone not here... What was Dan doing studying the group on Archers Road? What was he writing down?

A horrible thought burned into my brain.

Did Dan rat us out? Like he threatened on the pier. He's going to sell me out.

I'm aware I can be paranoid at times, but this... this was something else. Instinct?

The man on the pier was a practice call. I'm going to be next. He's going to send me to jail, so he and Nikki can run off together.

Could Dan really be capable of that? He's too much of a coward.

I did threaten to tell Victor Romeo about his plans. And he hates your guts.

The car stopped.

We all stepped out onto the field. There was a circle of cars, all aiming their lights on a shadowy figure on the ground.

"I've called you all here to show you all. We don't take kindly to people who rat-on-us…" Leebee announced to the horde of people.

"If you grass. It'll be the last thing you ever do. And we will. We will. Always find you."

The flock all murmur among their own clicks. Leebee pulled out a gun from his back.

"An example must be made."

Leebee marched over towards me. My eyes were glued onto the black nine millimetre. There was crunching noise underneath Leebee's feet every time he took a step, and that crunching grew louder and louder as he came closer. He lifted the gun up, I flinched.

Leebee opened up the chamber to see if it was loaded. The click made me shiver. Then pulled out the clip… I saw them—golden bullets neatly stacked on top of each other. Leebee offered the gun to me.

"What do you want me to do?"

I asked, sheepishly. I'm not sure why. I know exactly what he wants me to do. Leebee put his arm around me. It was the first time I felt sickened by his touch.

"I want you to walk over there and put a bullet in his head."

I looked at the shadowy figure kneeling on the floor. The beams were too bright I can't make out who it is. All I could see, this person was on his knees, staring down the freshly dug hole in the ground. There was a lump in my throat, I struggled to speak.

"Who is he?"

Please don't be Dan. Please don't be Dan.

"Does it matter?"

"Why me?"

"It's time for you to step up, bruv. You're gonna be a lieutenant."

In the corner of my eye, I saw DC's jealousy.

"Why not DC?"

Leebee laughed, but it was unfunny.

"You wanna keep working on *dem* street corners? Or you wanna do some*ting* more?"

MORE. I've always wanted more. I'm tired of the late nights and early mornings. I want MORE money. MORE respect. DC might be mad now, but Leebee might be mad if I say no. What choice do I have? If I say no to Leebee now, he would kill me. If I say yes, then DC would kill me another time. That would be a problem I would have to deal with later.

I took the gun. It felt heavy in my hands, also *cold*.

"It's gotta be done," Leebee ordered.

DC stepped in, he couldn't contain his envy any longer.

"Boy's a pussy-hole, he's not gonna do it. He's a waste man."

"I'll do it," I reluctantly agreed.

I drift over to the shadowy figure. The field fell silent. Everyone's eyes were on me.

Don't know if I can do this?

As I got nearer to Dan, images of our childhood came to mind... *The Lightsabre Fights... the den that we built in the woods... the promise we made on the beach... "we'll always be best friends."* He was always so smart, and so fast. This is how his life is coming to an end—shot and buried in a ditch.

He's my best friend. I can't shoot him in the head.

Tears dripped from my eyes, I haven't felt myself cry in a long time.

When I got closer to Dan, all I could hear was muffled weeping. He was stripped naked, the cold was making his shaking skin blue. That wasn't his biggest problem. His problem was me, and the grave he's just dug. His hands, mouth, and eyes were covered in duct tape. I didn't need to peel off the sticky tape to see who it was.

It's not Dan.

It came as a relief, but I have no idea who this person is. It might be best not to have known. Still, who am I to bring this man to his fate, so early?

Don't think about it. Just switch off and pull the trigger.

Everyone else was growing impatient. They want me to hurry up so they can go home and go to bed.

I stood behind the man, lifted the gun, my hand shook. The barrel pointed towards the back of the man's head. I swayed so much that the tip of the nine millimetre pressed against the guy's hair. He felt it. The whimpering became a muffled scream. Shit. That's not what I wanted.

It was hard to hear what he was yelling, but underneath the tape, I heard a '*pleeease*'.

I switched off until I was numb inside.

"I'm sorry."

It was either you or me.

In a flash of light… it was over.

I forgot about the recoil, I had jumped back two spaces. As I trudged back towards the *Range Rover,* it felt like I had left a part of me. Sounds of shovels in dirt began to fade in the distance. A stranger was not the only thing buried there. I felt the need to be sick. Some vomit raised in my mouth, but the rest I managed to press down.

"Well done, bruv," Leebee smiled.

I was still happy to gain his approval. Seeing DC so furious made me smug. He hates that I have proved him wrong and succeeded.

"Who was he?" I asked again.

Leebee huddled me, DC, and Darnell in a circle. Our leader actually replied to my question this time.

"He was the one who got Mickey arrested last year."

I recalled seeing Mickey being bent over police care and placed in handcuffs.

Darnell looked confused. "So who got our man on the pier arrested?"

"I don't know," Leebee replied.

"But no one else can know, that we don't know. *Dis* stays between us."

Dan. It was Dan. My first instinct was right. He's too smart to get caught.

Just before I stepped into the vehicle a hand grabbed my shoulder, spun me around. DC had shoved me against the car, putting his hands around my blue-collar.

"I bet it was fucking you, man. You were the one who called the pigs. I know you're not one of us."

"Get off me."

Darnell rushed in and separated DC from me.

"What's *dis* about, blud?"

DC walked off in a tantrum, crying like a fat spoilt brat.

"It's supposed to me. It's my chance to step up. Not this fucking cunt."

"Your time will come."

Leebee reassured, but I bet he's lying. No one wants DC to be in charge. He's too much of a hothead.

"When I find out Joe is a snake. I will put a bullet in right his fucking head."

DC slobbered from his fat red face when he screamed.

I'd grown tired of being disrespected by DC. This was a good time and place to show Leebee the voice recording on my phone. The one where Sticks admits to him and DC stealing cookies from the jar.

Before I did that, I prepared for the recoil and used the gun from my back pocket to put DC down. I was aiming for his head, but I got his shoulder, chest and then finally I got a bullet in the middle of his forehead. Parts of his mushy, tiny brain spread all over the grass. Darnell, Sticks and Leebee were like frightened rabbits. They were too shocked to move.

"Give me the gun," Leebee commanded.

I followed the instruction and willingly gave our leader the gun by the handle. Presenting it as a gift. Once Leebee had the gun, I raised my hands in surrender.

"Let me explain. DC and Sticks have been stealing from you. I have evidence on my phone."

"Show me."

I slowly raised my hand into my pocket, grabbed my phone and played the message.

He, Sticks, and Darnell heard it all right up to me asking, *"So it's alright for you and DC to steal but not that boy?"* Then Sticks replying, *"Der's a difference, bruv. Leebee doesn't know anythin' 'bout mine and DC's shit."*

Sticks looked like he just shit in his pants.

"I don't know what any of that is."

145

Leebee was furious, he pointed the gun at Sticks's head.

"Away from the car."

Sticks raised his hands, circled away from the car. Maintaining a watchful eye on the barrel of the gun.

"Listen, yeah. I promise I won't steal from you again. It was DC's idea. You can trust me, fam."

Leebee pulled the trigger. The gunshot echoed throughout the air. Sticks bled out on the floor, he was left to die slowly. Sticks rolled the dirt in agony, unable to stand up from the bullet wound in his chest.

Leebee grabbed me by the shoulder and yelled in my ear.

"You do not shoot one of my guys without my promotion. Understand me?"

"Yes, I do."

"The next time you do. You'll be digging your own grave next."

"I understand."

"Darnell, you've gotta drive."

Darnell went over to Stick's pocket to get the keys. By the time he walked over to our ex-driver. Sticks were out cold, as stiff as a board.

Leebee let me off easy.

"Joe, as punishment, you'll be left out here on ya own. You've gotta dig their graves."

He nods to the corpses of DC and Sticks.

"Then after, you've gotta walk back home. Burn the shovels. Be at work tomorrow."

Everybody left. Leaving me to dig the graves of two of my biggest problems. I wouldn't get home till the sun rises, but it would be worth it.

The walk home was tough. I felt sick, but I did not feel remorse. The world is probably better off without DC or Sticks. Not too sure about that other guy. Normally, there would be a voice in my head.

That voice would say some*ting* like, "Why did you kill that innocent man, Joe?" It was not there. That voice, that good angel on my shoulder, was silenced. It too had been buried underneath the dirt with that innocent guy. I thought it was best to move on. Nothing good comes from thinking about the past.

Besides, it's not my fault. I knew whose fault it was. The blame goes to the person who called the cops on our boy on the pier. If that didn't happen, then we wouldn't have to make an example by killing that bloke.

That person should have never called the cops. I wonder who it was… *What was Dan writing in his notebook? The times and location of my whereabouts to get me arrested. He's tested the waters on the dealer on the seafront… Am I next?*

Not if I put a stop to his plans first.

Chapter 37

Dan

"It worked."

I almost felt giddy, like a schoolboy, again.

"The police actually arrested the drug dealer by the seafront. Tell me, was the car here last night?" I asked Nikki.

"No, they must have called an emergency meeting, or something, after you called the cops."

She smiled. How I had missed her beam. Colour would have returned to her cheeks if she wasn't wearing so much white face powder.

"We have to be more careful now."

Her tone was more cautious, and it was one of reason—a reminder to not get too carried away.

"What you are saying is true. Next time I make an anonymous phone call to the authorities, it will be the details of Joe's crew on Archers Road and the high street dealer. There would be a second emergency meeting or they'll be too occupied chasing their own tails. Then me, you, and little Alfie can jump in my uncle's car and drive to Hampshire."

"We still have one week to go, Dan. Does anybody else know about the operation?"

"Yes… Joe."

Nikki's face dropped.

"Why did you tell him?"

"Believe me, I had to."

Our voices raised, causing my head to throb.

"What if he tells Leebee?"

"He's my best friend."

"He won't be when you call the cops on him."

She had a good point.

"What if we pretend to break up?"

"It's not going to work, Dan."

"Damn it, we have to try."

I believed I had this under control, I paced up down the bedroom trying to conjure more ideas. The migraine kept interfering, blocking out any new thoughts.

"You've screwed this up when you told Joe."

"At least I'm fucking doing something."

The baby began to cry.

"Oh, well done, you've just woke up Alfie."

Nikki leant over the cot. Embraced Alfie in her loving arms. Cradled the boy gently while he cried in the warmth of her black hoodie.

"*Ssshhh… Ssshhh*. It's okay, it's okay."

I never imagined I could yell at Nikki as loud or as deep. A dark malicious voice came from somewhere within. The baby's screams only intensified my headache. I rub my temples vigorously while Nikki stares daggers onto me, with eyes that can only say… *Great work, Dan. Look at what you've done… you've upset Alfie.*

"Nikki, I'm sorry for yelling. It's just been stressful."

"It's been hard for me as well."

I sit on the edge of her bed, in shame. After taking steady breaths to suppress that angry voice within me. My head was now on fire. The sunlight from the window did not help the situation. In the corner of my eye, a ray of sunlight reflects on a round cylinder object. Tucked away, behind the bedpost. I picked it up, it was a wine bottle. No. A *hidden* wine bottle.

Who else used to hide alcohol, Dan? You know who… your mother.

"What's this?"

"Oh, it's, *erm*. Just some wine. I have a glass before bed."

"Why is it hidden underneath your bed?"

Nikki nervously bit her lip. Her shameful eyes turned away from mine.

"Sometimes I do like a glass, it helps me get to sleep."

"What about Alfie?"

"He's not old enough to drink." She spouted nervous laughter. Even though it was not remotely funny.

"How much do you drink? Once a week? Once every other day? Every night? Do you get the shakes in the morning? Do you drink because you really want to get so drunk, that you forget you ever had a bastard son, to begin with?"

My head exploded. The deep dark bitter voice roared out of the pit it had been buried inside of me. It was more malevolent than ever. Nikki's tears ran alongside Alfie's.

"What? Why would you say that?"

My red face is now screaming in hers.

"I know people like you. You disgust me. You're going to be a terrible mum. You'll neglect him. Forget to feed him. He'll grow up to be as damaged as you. Someone who'll grow up to, literally, fuck anyone or anything. Even a fucking psychopath. Why would I ever imagine that someone like me, would choose a silly, idiotic, stupid, poor, slag, like you?"

"Get out! I want you out of this house. Right now. Never come round here again. I hate you."

If Nikki had not have been holding a crying Alfie, I'm sure she would have scratched my eyes out on my way out.

I marched home, slammed the front door upon arrival. My mother had been waiting for me. Her hunched body shook. One of her claws is wielding the whisky bottle. Her spiteful face growled at my presence.

"What?"

The flab pointing out her small pink shirt flapped as she wobbled towards me.

"You know what? After all, I've done for you."

Sigh "You're hallucinating again. Why don't I make you coffee and you call it a night?"

I shoulder-barged past the beast, entered the kitchen through the living room. Placed my hand in the bowl of murky cold washing up water, to fish out a mug.

My mother chased me holding a letter in her hand. Wafting it in my face.

"What's that?"

"You know what this is," she shrieked.

"No."

"It's a letter saying you've been offered a place in a school in Hampshire."

"You've read my mail?"

"Yes because I knew you've been up to something. Do you think I'm stupid? Ha. Ha."

She slaps me on the side of my head.

"And who the hell is Nikki Yakes? Why is she going with you? Why is she pregnant to your child?"

She raises her two claws by the side of her ragged face. Hisses like a snake, then scratches her long sharp claws down my arm, over and over again. Like a cat digging its way into the chest cavity of a mouse.

"Now look what you've done."

She accuses me of dropping the mug on purpose.

"Fuck sake mum. You crazy bitch."

"Oooh. I'mmmm crazy. You think I'm crazy do ya?"

Her eyes were wild.

"How about this for crazy? I'm not fucking crazy because you're the one that's crazy. You selfish, horrible, little child. I gave up everything to raise you up. This is how you repay me? By ditching me to go to *Hampshire. Wellll*, you're not going. You know you need to stay here and look after your mother."

"No, mum. I've had enough. All my life, I've done nothing but take care of you. When you are supposed to be caring for me."

My eyes began to burn.

"Why can't you just be like any other mum?"

"You best not be defying me. I am your mother. You will do as I say."

"No, mum, I'm going. I'm going to take Nikki with me… because I love her."

"She'll just leave you. Or use you. I mean who would want to be with an *ugly, skinny, selfish* shit, like you?"

I couldn't control my relentless crying. But I could control my situation with my mother. Tired of the odour from her mouth being so close to my face, I pushed her away.

"Goodbye, mum."

"You're not leaving me, alone."

"You deserve to be alone."

151

She grabbed me by my hair, pushed my head into the bowl of murky water. I felt the blade of a used knife slashing the side of my cheek. My lungs gasped for air. Instead, I was inhaling more dishwater. My eyes stung. My arms flapped around, as I tried to push her to hold over me. Eventually, she yanked my head from the bowl. I breathed… temporarily. The beast wrapped her talons around my neck, shoved me against the wall. With some strength, she had lifted me up from the ground, feet dangling from the floor.

"Say that again," she hissed.

"Fuck you," I garbled.

I noticed a plate was hanging from the edge of the counter. I stretched out my arm. With the tips of my fingers tapped the edge of the surface. It rattled towards the centre of my palm. Then I got more of a grip. I smashed the plate on the side of my mother's head. She yelped as tumbled to the floor. My lungs were so thankful to breathe, they tried to absorb too much air at once, causing me to cough. My mum laid on the floor, in and around broken shards. Blood-stained her thick blonde hair.

Thankfully, she was still breathing. That's how she was when I left her. I grabbed my bag and left. Never to return.

Chapter 38

Joe

I waited till Gareth Hall was alone. Even during the school hols, his office was still open.

The shrink has just finished talking to another weak boy. Gareth picked up some papers, ready to bounce. I took my chance.

"Yo, bruv."

The doc had almost dropped all his papers. He looked startled.

"Oh. Hi there. How can I help you?"

Gareth placed out a box of tissues, he had previously packed away.

I won't be needing any of dem, bruv.

I giggled.

"Come in. Close the door."

"I won't be here long. You know about Dan Suddlemire, going to some posh school in Hampshire?"

Gareth had given me the beady eyes.

"What about it?"

"You know he's taking Nikki Yakes and her daughter?"

"I believed it to be Daniel and Nikki's daughter."

I burst out laughing. I never have I once dreamed Dan could lie like *dat*.

"No, bruv. Do you know who Victor Romeo is?"

"The name does ring a bell."

He knows. Every man and his dog know.

"Nikki Yake's son *is* Victor Romeo's grandson. The baby is not Dan's fam'."

His smile had an edge to it. Even though he wants to be friendly, really he be brickin' it.

"I am pretty sure you are pulling my leg, Mr… what's your name again?"

"Never mind about me, bruv. You gotta look out for number one. If Romeo finds out, what ya done. You're gonna be a dead man."

I knew he'd set up the accommodation for Dan and Nikki. He's gonna be in some serious shit when Victor Romeo finds out. So it's best to warn him. For his sake… no one else's.

Chapter 39

Dan

"I need your help."

Gareth was startled when I approached him. I was not sure what staggered him more—was it the cuts on my face and arm? The fact that I surprised him at the school's car park? Perhaps it was the fact I've just asked for his help?

"Daniel. Are you okay? What happened to you?"

"I have nowhere to go."

Gareth scanned the car park to see if anyone was watching.

"Get in. You can crash at mine."

"Are you sure? This feels a little unorthodox."

"Yes. Quickly before someone sees."

That astonished me. I knew I could rely on his kindness because he always went the extra mile for his clients. However, I didn't think he would do something that could make him lose his licence. Or worse… go to jail over.

There's something off about this.

What choice did I have? Joe hates me, and Nikki currently despises me.

In the car, I told him about all the dreadful things I'd said to Nikki. How I wished I could take them back. Then proceeded to tell Gareth about the fight with my mum, and how I'd run away from home.

"Are you going to call social services?"

He paused.

"You're going to Hampshire in a few days. If you were permanently homeless, then yes I would. Tonight, you can sleep on my settee, then we'll see what tomorrow brings us."

Something's not settling right, Dan.

I was too exhausted to argue with my internal self and felt too fragile to sleep on the streets.

"I would call my Uncle Clive, but I don't have my mobile phone."

"Are you close to your uncle?"

"Very. He's actually my granddad, but he hates the word 'granddad'. He lives in the north of England. I need to find his mobile."

"Is he listed in the *Yellow Pages*?"

"I think so. Does anyone still use them?"

"I have the last issue."

Gareth had one of the few single-detached houses. I was even envious of his front drive. He could afford such luxuries as a doctor. However, if I had his money I wouldn't move into this area. It's prone to burglaries.

The house might blossom on the outside, but the interior did not look like how I would imagine… *a home.* The walls were painted in a dull grey emulsion. Nothing hung on the walls. No ornaments, no family photos, or any sign of life. The living room had one double settee beside the occupied bookshelf.

"No TV."

What kind of person doesn't own a television?

The kitchen table could only cater for one person. The sink was full of unwashed dishes. I opened the freezer, and as I suspected, it was full of microwave meals for one.

"Would you like something to eat?" My stomach rumbled, but I thought about Gareth, slipping some drugs into my food or drinks. Whilst I'm unconscious he would sexually assault me, or surgically remove one of my kidneys.

"No, thanks. It's not that I'm ungrateful for your hospitality, but why are you helping me?"

He leant back on his own dining table, used his index finger to adjust his glasses.

"I believe you're a good kid. Who has been handed a shit deal at the start of your life? From your father leaving you, to having to look after your alcoholic, abusive mother, to being bullied. You could be classed as a genius, but none of your lazy teachers has been bothered to detect your talents. Yet there's a part in your, what I call, the adult brain. And it says, 'don't revert to childlike behaviours, such as obsessive-compulsive disorders and addiction."

"Are you *Sigmund Freud* now?"

"I don't believe in all his work, but his initial idea was the foundation for all other psychologists in the world. I believe you want to do the right thing. Many other factors in this world have made you into several different characters, in order to cope with these factors."

"I'm lost."

"Do you recall your third or fourth session? You said, 'I feel so numb. If I cut my wrist, I'm not sure anything would bleed out.' Can you remember what I did next?"

"You said, 'why don't you go ahead and do it?' Then you pulled out a pocket knife and stuck it on the table. Leaving it there."

I recall it being unconventional.

"Because I knew you were too sensible to do it. What *Freud* called your '*super-ego*' is what I call your 'maturer personal'. That maturer personal, or what some call *The Adult Brain*, is your rational self."

"Like my consciousness?"

"Exactly. That's the part of your brain that tells you what you're thinking or doing is wrong."

"It sounded crazy, saying it out loud."

"Sometimes hearing your own dark and twisted thoughts out loud can make you realise it sounds outrageous. Can you recollect your eighth session? You mentioned how *Frank Turner's* music made you want to be a better person. You know: *'Be More Kind', 'Get Better'* or *'I Still Believe'*. A part of you wants to believe in these ideals. You want to be more kind to others, get better at yourself, and be a more hopeful person. However, seeing the cruel people on the mean streets, and in your home, has only made you want to be a cold and defensive person. Because if you were that, the tough, uncaring type, then you wouldn't get hurt."

"Is this the root cause of my anxiety?"

"Possibly. Different parts of you have their own individual 'needs', and those 'needs' are not being met."

"What about the visions?"

"They're still suppressed rage."

"How can you remember all of this?"

"Daniel, you forget. I have been your councillor for almost a year. Also, I'm a good listener."

He smiles.

"Why have you stuck by me all this time?"

"Because you needed help. This is why I'm here—to help."

"You could get into a lot of trouble sheltering me for the night."

"I know you can keep a secret."

Guilt was a heavy debt. I owe Gareth so much, and how did I repay him? By lying to him, telling him Alfie was my biological child. Now the school in Hampshire made special arrangements to accommodate me, Nikki and Alfie. My head was heavy, and there was a piece of hot burning charcoal sitting in my stomach, destroying me from the inside.

"Do you mind if I go to bed early? I'm tired."

"It's only 7:00 p.m.?"

"I know, I just want to be alone."

"Feel free to explore my bookshelf."

"Thank you. Where is your phone?"

"The landline and phone book is by the front door."

"Sorry, '*land... line*'? Next, you'll be telling me you have a fax machine."

Gareth chuckles.

"I do. I also save my work onto *floppy disks.*"

I pretended to laugh at his joke, but I had no idea what he was referring to.

Before I went to bed, I left a voicemail on my Uncle C's answering machine. Asking if he could pick me up from this current address the following day? Also, I needed somewhere to stay. I would have got the train up if I had some money. All I had with me are my keys, my tight black *Placebo* shirt, skinny black jeans, and the holey trainers.

I woke up in the unfamiliar dark room. The half-opened book *Haunted* by James Herbert had fallen onto the floor. With being dazed and half asleep, it took me time to gather my bearings.

Where am I?

I was laying on Gareth's settee. I knew this because I could hear his voice on the landing. The door is slightly ajar. I see the psychiatrist on his mobile.

"Yes... Yes... Sure... No. I won't let that happen."

158

Who is he talking to?

Gareth peeped through the gap of the door. I shut my eyes, pretending to be asleep.

"No. No… The boy is in my custody for the night."

That's all I heard. He took the rest of the conversation outside.

Was he talking about me? Who was he talking to? My mum? The school?

Questions raced through my mind. I had a feeling the answers would come soon.

Told you coming here was a mistake.

Best stay awake, keep my guard up. Do not fall asleep.

Chapter 40

Dan

The morning dawned. I woke, disorientated. I must have dropped off for a short while.

"The boy is in my custody for the night."

Shit. I remembered I need to get out of here.

If you run, Gareth might cancel your scholarship or the accommodation, or both.

The internal voice in my head sounds like Nikki now. Who knew that she would ever be the voice of reason? Maybe I just miss her.

"Good afternoon, sleepyhead."

Afternoon? How long have I been asleep?

"What time is it?"

I ask while wiping the sleep from my eyes.

"It's almost ten."

"Has my uncle called back?"

"Not yet."

There was a sense that he could be lying. I should know, I'm the greatest liar there is.

Although, Uncle C isn't the best, or quickest, telecommunicator.

"I need to go to the butchers to pick up some meat. Do you want to come with me?"

This is my chance to escape.

"No, I best take my leave. I have already taken so much of your hospitality."

"Well, it's on the way to the train station. Would you like to be dropped off?"

"That would be great, thank you."

"Do you have any money for the train?"

"No, I'll jump on."

"That's a risky move."

"I don't know what else to do."

He stares at me, worryingly. Eventually, he agrees. I think he would like to treat me like a son.

Until his 'Maturer Personal' realises that I am not his son—and never will be.

The rusty bell above the door jingles, alerting everyone in the butchers to our presence. Why am I following Gareth inside? I am secretly wanting some food. Is this what my life has come to—scrounging?

The grumpy, overweight man behind the counter is not the friendliest of greeters. His dark eyes do not leave my sight. Just in front of his blood-soaked apron, the butcher sharpens one knife with another. The continuous swiping of the blades pierces through the air, making me shudder. Gareth stepped to the counter, but he never spoke. The butcher stops swiping the knives, although he remains chillingly silent. Both butcher and psychiatrist engage in a bizarre staring competition. An eerie quietness descends upon the room. Until…

"Ah, they are here."

A voice reverberates from the back room. Someone steps out from the clear PVC-striped curtains. My face turned white. My heart stopped. It was the last person I wanted to see…

Victor Romeo.

I don't know what the crime boss was doing in the backroom, but he had to wear an apron. In order to protect his expensive suit from the blood splatter. This could be an act to scare you, Dan. Act or not, if his intention is to frighten me. It's definitely working. Romeo giggles as he unknots his apron. He straightens his tie then rubs his hands together. He ogles at me with hungry eyes, while simultaneously licking his lips. It was as if the big bad wolf has brought in the sheep for the slaughter.

"Sit down, Daniel."

Chapter 41
Joe

Me, Leebee and Darnell drove past the 'You are now leaving Desby' sign. At least this was on a clearer day. In my experience, driving during the day was a more positive experience than a night drive.

Darnell had involuntarily become Leebee's personal driver. It was the three of us. No more DC or Sticks that could stop me from getting to the top.

The ride took us to a new estate. At the entrance was the face of the main man himself, Victor Romeo. Victor had bought the land, built the houses, and charged the tenants a fortune. You only needed a small deposit for the mortgage. When you're finally able to pay off the mortgage you will still have to pay a monthly fee to Romeo. We parked on the freshly paved bright red cobblestoned path.

"This house is massive," Darnell pointed out.

He was not wrong. I gazed upon the bright single-detached house. It was nothing like the terraced houses, the best semi-detached, or the high-rises in Desby. This house, and every other house on the street, was an ultra-modern red brick home. With a small patch of fake grass on the front with a single plastic tree on the front. A smooth, brown uPVC door was at the front porch. The porch was next to a freshly painted white garage door.

"Let's take a look inside," Leebee suggested.

Leebee took me for a tour, while Darnell waited by the car. Stepping in was like being in another world. It was so posh and bright. The kitchen was epic. Underneath the stainless steel worktops, were oak cabinets. The kitchen island had four matching brown stools.

The long conservatory-type door and window spread across the entire back wall. The garden was proper good. The dining room had just one long table. The living room had a single cream settee facing a thirty-two-inch TV. The floor was made of polished floor tiles, but there was a soft furry-rug-thingy to keep your feet warm.

Imagine if I lived here. I could bring as many girls back as I want. No longer will I have to be ashamed of living in a small place.

"You like it, bruv?" Leebee asked.

"It's fucking awesome."

"It's yours, man."

That never really sunk in, I needed to hear that again.

"What did you say?"

"It's yours, bruv. The whole fucking house."

I laughed.

"You can't be serious."

"Victor Romeo is proppa impressed by you. He wants you to have it. It's a reward for stepping up."

I can't shake off the shock. It still felt like a dream.

"What do I have to do?"

"Just stay 'ere and look after the house. Keep it clean and dat."

What's the catch?

Leebee continued, "There'll be some people calling in every now and then. It might be once a week. It might be on a Tuesday and Thursday. The times will keep changing. They'll give you some things to look after. Money, crack, or they might need to leave a car in the garage for a while."

They also might need to use the table in the dining room to cut up some shit.

"That's what that long table is for."

"Any problems, ring this number."

He gave me another burner.

"It's a pay-as-you-go. Only enough for one phone call. Afterwards, get rid of it. Follow me?"

"I do."

"I know you do. You've done good, fam."

"When do I move in?"

"Tomorrow."

No more late nights. No more early morning runs. No more dodging the police on the street. No more murders. I've finally made it. My dream of living in a nice house, in a nice hood, is here.

I've never been so happy.

What about Dan? What about the promise you made?

Fuck, Dan. He was going to fuck me over and turn me into the pigs. He broke the promise first by taking Nikki to Hampshire.

They probably won't make it to Hampshire now.

Whatever happens to him now… is on him.

Chapter 42

Dan

I turned towards the door, to run. There was a military-grade bodyguard, one who resembled *Henry Rollins*, barricading the door.

"I said, 'sit down' Daniel."

Victor's tone was more forceful.

I sit on the plastic chairs, Gareth follows me. Forcing me to sit against the wall, further form the door. Not my first choice.

"Daniel Suddlemire. I know what you are planning to do."

I gaze upon a sullen Gareth with pleading eyes. My eyes say "Why have you done this, Gareth? Why have you betrayed me?" Of course, he's betrayed me. I should have known better than to trust other people.
"I wouldn't blame Gareth, Mr Suddlemire. You should be thankful you have someone so caring on your side."

Victor Romeo sat opposite me and reached into the inner blazer pocket to pull out an envelope.

"I have always known about your relationship with Nikki."

He pulls out a selection of photographs and spreads them across the table. There was one of me and Nikki going to the free birthing class at the community hall. One of me, Nikki, and the baby having a picnic at the park on a hot summer day. A polaroid of me outside Nikki's house, holding a broken nose. I gaze at the rest of the intrusive photographs. *whack*

I leapt out of my skin, as the butcher chops something tender with his meat cleaver. My heart races so much that the rush of adrenaline sends me into flight mode. However, I'm trapped here. Here in the corner between the traitorous Gareth and the interrogating Romeo. The walls are closing in around me. I feel myself shrinking, smaller and smaller.

Why's it getting so hot in here?

Victor Romeo continues to stare at me.

"Do you really think you could steal my grandson away from me? How do you think you would be able to run to Hampshire without me knowing?"

I try to speak, but I stumble over my own words.

"I understand. I grew up here in Desby. I too had to fight to survive. I made a promise to myself: 'when I grow up, I'm going to make something of myself.' And that's what I did. I got to the top. Isn't that what you want to do? Leave this town and be a better version of yourself? Me and you, we're the same…"

I'm nothing remotely like you.

"We grew up in this shit hole. But we are better than this town, and the people in it."

I manage to speak without sounding so timid.

"Your money could help boost the economy. You could have made it a better place."

"My money *is* the economy of this town. Without my money in its banks, then this seaside resort would really be a ghost town. That's one of the reasons why I am untouchable. That's one of the reasons why you are here, Dan."

I feel a proposition is going to be offered.

"Come and work for me. You wouldn't be one of those idiots on the streets, selling shit. You'll help me with my finances, as an accountant. Gareth tells me you're great with numbers. Gifted, even. While no one else will acknowledge your abilities, I will reward them."

I would be lying if I said I wasn't interested.

"I will pay for your university fee, I will give you a brand new house in one of my new estates. In return, you offer me your loyalty."

A dark selfish part wanted me to agree.

You can finally leave Desby. You could get a job that uses your abilities. Live in a nice big house, in a nice safe street.

My thoughts turn to Nikki, Alfie, and even Joe.

Joe hates you. The blood pact is redundant.
"What about Nikki and Alfie?"

"You seem like a nice kid. And girls like Nikki… don't really know what they want. If you catch my drift? They need nice boys to keep them right. She deserves someone like you. But my grandson stays with me."

"I don't know. I want to protect Alfie."

"How could you protect Alfie? You're just a boy. A skinny arse white boy, with no contacts. I know that I've failed with Joel. A regret I will take with me to my grave. I need someone to take over my empire when I'm gone. I thought it would be Joel, but that moron couldn't even handle a simple school fight. I will do better this time."

Nikki wouldn't go through it. Notwithstanding the fact she loathes me.

Gareth eventually spoke. "It sounds like a good offer."

At this time, I don't think Gareth could say anything that wouldn't make me resent him less.

"As I said before, you are lucky to have someone like Gareth supporting you…"

Victor chuckles to his own memory.

"This guy really cares about the kids in his care. Do you know what he did?"

"No."

Gareth's face widens as he shakes his head. The petrified eyes behind his thick glasses yell… *Don't tell him. He doesn't need to know.*

Victor dismisses his plea, "A kid who was getting beaten badly by his stepdad. You might know him, he lives around here, works for me? No? Anyway, he came to Gareth a year and a half ago. Gareth lost his shit. Smashed in the stepdad's knees with a hammer."

Victor found all this amusing. Yet, Gareth appears to be regretful.

"Gareth was unemployed, and about to go to jail. I sorted it all out for him. I like to look after my friends."

Victor flashes a white, over-friendly smile to the remorseful psychologist. Gareth returns a spiteful glare. Gareth's resentful face helps me reach a decision. If I say yes to Victor Romeo's offer, I will always be in his debt.

"Dan, you have twenty-four hours to make your decision. I'll be here at 10:00 a.m. tomorrow. It might be in your best interest to say yes. If I don't see you, I'll assume your answer's no."

Henry Rollins opened the door for us.

167

The drive back to Gareth's is a quiet one. The car slows to a halt outside his house. I couldn't contain my rage anymore.

"Why did you do it? Why did you tell Victor Romeo?"

"I had to. He employed me to go to the school to find out what Joel's classmates knew about the stabbing, and what Joel had been saying about Victor's operation. Also, to see if any of the younger recruits were blabbing to the police."

"You knew I was seeing Nikki Yakes for months."

"I didn't know she was Joel's sidepiece. Besides, you told me the baby was yours. The school wasn't happy about making special arrangements for you. But I convinced them to, and sent them a generous donation."

"I didn't ask you to do that."

"But that's what you wanted. I really meant it when I said I wanted to help."

"You've ruined everything for Nikki, and Alfie."

"He was going to find out anyway. It was either me talking to him, or you end up dead somewhere. Trust me, I don't prefer the latter."

"I had it under control."

"You are just a seventeen-year-old kid, Dan. You can't handle this on your own."

I unbuckle my seatbelt and leave the car.

In Gareth's house. I check to see if Uncle Clive has left a message on the phone. There was none. Gareth marched into the kitchen. Opened a bottle of whiskey and drank it neat. Letting the burning sensation poison any feelings of guilt. He threw his wallet and keys onto the table before storming upstairs, bottle in hand. I heard the shower water running. I took this opportunity to reach my hand inside his wallet and steal all the notes from within. Whilst on the looting spree, I pilfer one of his kitchen knives, for protection purposes. There is only one person who knew about mine and Nikki's scheme to run away… and that person needs to pay for it.

Chapter 43
Joe

Sick and tired of these fucking junkies, man. Their ageing faces make me sick. Sick of them trying to negotiate the spice. Tired of them hanging around me like flies. I'm so glad this is my last night. I am going to miss some of the boys I've been working with. Not all. Most are a set of hard cunts that don't give a fuck about anyone. It's time to move on to bigger and better *tings*.

You best start saying 'THINGS' rather than 'tings'. If you want to blend in the new nice neighbourhood. Otherwise, people will notice that you don't belong there.

I best come up with a story. To let the nosey snobs know why I am able to afford the house... I could tell them it's my parents' house. My mum and her new boyfriend Rick work away a lot. Which isn't a complete lie.

My mum's new boyfriend is a fireman, *Fireman Sam* I like to call him. He is mainly based in London. She met him on *Tinder*. After a few dates, she's practically moved in with him. Leaving me behind.

That's okay as I'm an adult now. I have my own life, job, and now I have my own mansion. We still text every day, but it's not the same. I still think of her and love her, but the chord's been cut—it's time to grow up.

It's two in the morning. My last shift has come to an end... it's over.

Until I hear multiple voices from behind me.

"What you *tink* you doing, blud?"

"Fuck off, man."

"If you ain't buying shit, step off."

What was the commotion? Behind me, some of the boys circle around some bloke. I can't see who it is from the many heads in the way.

"I just want to speak to Joe," the voice cried.

"Look at him, he's like a proppa crackhead, in' he?" one guy jokes.

"I'm not going anywhere until you let me see Joe."

My curiosity got the better of me,

"Allow."

The crowd parts. Dan's miserable face looks at me.

"What do you want?" I grudged.

"I've spent all night looking for you."

"Well, you've found me."

The rest of the crew look like they're gonna pounce on my old friend.

"Give us a minute," I commanded.

The gang gave us some space. It was only Dan… What could he do to hurt me?

"Joe…"

He plods closer to me.

"I know what you have done."

I watch as he puts his hand behind his back.

"What have you got there?" I asked.

"Why did you do it? Do you hate me that much?"

His eyes were turning red. I hope he doesn't cry again.

"You were gonna sell me out. I saw you, studying what I wa' doing. You called the police on our guys, as a taster. You wanna see if it worked—"

"You're being paranoid, you always were—"

He steps closer, I leap back.

"And you're lying, Dan. You've always been a snake. You were going to call the force. Probably so you and Nikki could escape. I can't go to jail, Dan. You left me no choice. This is on you."

"You're right… I did."

Hearing him confess, only made me hate him more. I felt my eyes burn red, but with rage rather than tears. I am turning into a bull, and Dan is now the red flag. There was a sense to charge at him, take him down to the ground… and kill him.

"I'm sorry. Let me make it right. You're right this is my fault. It was my selfishness that started our rivalry. Let me make it up to you. Let's put all of this behind us…"

I thought Dan was going to get on his hands and knees and grovel. That would be a sight to see.

"I have some money. I can get a train up north, grab my uncle's car, and we'll drive out of this town *together*."

I ain't goin' anywhere wit' you.

"It's what I should have done. A long time ago."

I burst out laughing, "I don't need your help anymore. I'm leavin' *dis* town. Tomorrow, I'm gonna be gone."

Dan was confused. He doesn't know.

"What are you talking about?"

"I mean, I ain't gonna need you anymore. I have a nice house, in a new *safe* estate. It's funny 'cause, I've moved out of this shithole before you. *You* with all your brains. I'm making more money *den* you ever will."

Dan appears crushed. I step nearer to see the hurt in his eyes. To rub salt in the wound, I whisper in his big ears,

"Who's the smart one now?"

"I'm trying to save you."

"I don't need saving. It's you who's gonna need saving if you don't walk away right now."

Dan was pissing his pants.

"Are you going to kill me, Joe?"

"I've killed everyone else that has got in my way."

Dan walks away, admitting defeat. I was almost proud of him—he didn't cry. He's becoming a man. He saw something in my eyes… the light in my baby blue eyes has gone.

Chapter 44

Dan

The sparkle in Joe's baby blue eyes has gone. The innocence inside has been murdered, along with other people. Joe is not capable of murder. But, the person I was speaking to last night, was not Joe. Joe, the little boy who used to love climbing trees. The eleven-year-old, who I rode bikes with to the beach. The ten-year-old, who danced in his room to the music of *The Enemy.* He was gone. Replaced with a vicious imitation. The skin on the outer shell may resemble Joe Smith, but the interior parts are pumped by cold venomous black blood. He's a monster.

I walk around aimlessly, from the boarded houses on Archers Road to the park. I will take one last look at the old house, the High Street, the school gates, and finally to the seafront. I grab hold of the rusty black rails, feel the wind blow through my hair, listen to the water's gentle motion and watch the sunrise from the distant ocean. The sound of flocking seagulls on the dark gold sand, and the smell of the salty sea air, made me reminisce.

Happier times. Simpler times. When it was just me and Joe on the beach. Two young friends playing on the beach. We could have grown up to be blessed and untroubled... but the adult world will not allow such a thing.

I now feel the sun glow upon my acne-free face. I bathed in the sun's glory for what could be the last time. As I know what to do to save Nikki and Joe. I devise two plans. One being the last resort. The first one should be easier... kill Victor Romeo.

Part 4 – There Are No Heroes or Villains; Just People

Chapter 45

Dan

I believe in monsters. Not like the ones in children's books. Monsters are people. People who thrive on violence and the suffering of others. These people have no conscience, they have no guilt, no remorse, nor do they seek any repentance. People such as Victor Romeo are monsters.

I crouch in the bushes, examining the butchers on the opposite side of the road. The only thing I'm missing is a pair of binoculars or a newspaper with two eye holes cut out. It's currently 8:00 a.m. (a stranger kindly gave me the time).

It's two hours before I'm supposed to go in there, get up close to Victor Romeo, then use Gareth's kitchen knife to cut the internal jugular vein and the carotid artery that runs along the side of his neck. It has to be done quickly—there is only one chance. Chances are I will not be walking out of the shop either. His bodyguard, *Henry Rollins* will shoot me down. But, that's okay. I will need to be put down, like a rabid dog. Once I do this, I too will become a monster.

In what feels like half an hour. A large black *Mercedes* parks near the butchers. Victor's bodyguard assistant opens the driver's seat for his boss. They both enter the shop. Another person enters the shop. On entry, this man gets patted down by *Henry Rollins*.

Shit. I didn't get searched last time.

How am I going to get this knife in the shop? Could I rearrange the meeting? Go in the shop before the next appointment and leave the knife somewhere hidden. So the next time I see Victor Romeo, I could get in the shop without the knife. No… that's not going to work because there isn't going to be another meeting after today.

I envision myself going in the shop clean. Then jump over the counter to grab the butcher's meat cleaver. However, the porky guy behind the counter grabs me, pins my skinny body against the wall. I try to worm my way free, but it is no use.

The butcher and guard drag me, nail and tooth, to the back room. Both pinning my body on a blood-soaked table. Victor Romeo licks his hungry lips and takes great delight by hacking my body into small pieces.

Entering the shop, I spread my arms out to be patted down by the sentinel's inked hands. He doesn't find anything because I've left the knife in the bushes. Victor Romeo greets me with a charming white smile. I walk up to the crime boss casually, grab him by his costly white shirt. He tries to fight me off. Victor throws himself towards me.

The crest of the table digs into my back. With all my strength, I flip him over. I am on top, but I panic. I don't know what I can use to kill him. Victor's hands dig into my neck and cheeks, trying to push me off. Whilst my hands are around his neck, pushing and squeezing.

With my one seeing eye, I spot a fork on the table. I aim to reach it. A sharp pain hits me in the side of the head. My body is no longer tense, all my muscles relax as I collapse to the floor. *Henry Rollins* stares at me, with a smoking barrel pointing in my direction. The white tiles are now splattered with my blood.

That's not going to work either.

Something like that will happen if I don't go in with a plan. I realise the chances of my survival are next to nothing, but Victor has to die first. Otherwise, my sacrifice will mean nothing.

I pace up and down the street trying to conjure a viable plan and envisage many scenarios in my head. Victor and his combative guard leave the shop.

I must have been taking too long.

I ran over to the opposite side of the road.

It's now or never.

174

The bodyguard notices someone's running towards them. With cat-like reflexes, he spins around. One hand is a virtual stop sign and the other hovers over his pistol holder.

"Hold it," he spoke firmly.

I am trying to stop on the spot, but like a car hitting the breaks when it's travelling too fast, I skid. The heels of my trainers could leave marks on the pavement.

Victor's face is the look of disapproval. I could almost feel the cold from his shoulder.

"You're too late, Daniel. The deal is off."

"Wait. Just hear me out," I pleaded.

Henry Rollins glaring eyes are narrowing.

"I would like to accept your offer, Mr Romeo." I stuck out my left hand.

"A tip for the future, do not turn up an hour late."

Just shut up and grab my hand.

Victor steps closer. My right-hand edges closer to the knife in my back pocket. My eyes jump back and forth from Romeo and his suspicious guard.

"I've lost my phone, so I wasn't sure what time it was."

"I have no room for excuses in my business," Romeo declared while edging closer.

My hand edges closer to the knife. My heart is beginning to race.

The bodyguard opens the pistol holder.

Victor begins to lecture me, "Daniel let me tell you something about the adult world…"

I no longer listen to his rough voice. There's a ringing in my ear. My head is pulsating. My right-hand touches the handle of the knife. My eyes drift towards the apprehensive bodyguard, his gun is out of the holder. His body is eager, ready to pounce and attack his prey.

I am not going to do it. Victor's too far away.

"…so if you ever come near me, or my grandson. I'll kill you and Joe Smith."

It took me a while to register the last part of Victor's threat.

"Wait. What did you say?"

"I know you and Joe Smith are close friends."

"We hate each other," I corrected.

"Yes, but you'd hate it for anything to happen to him."

"I'd rather see him dead than see him grow up to be like you."

Victor laughs, "You talk a great game. But you also have to walk the walk."

The crime boss stands further back. Realising that my target is now out of reach, I ease my right hand away from the weapon. However, *Henry Rollins* does not ease his trigger-happy hands.

"It's a shame, kid. You could have had a bright future," he sneers before entering the car.

Like a coward, I stand there and watch the *Mercedes* drive away. It feels like I am brought back down to reality. The adrenaline is dying. My eyes begin to cry. I am not sure why they're crying. I feel exhausted, meek, sad, and pathetic. I failed both Joe and Nikki.

Have I gone insane? Am I really ready to kill someone?

I lean over the drain to be sick.

Your life was already heading this way, Dan. This is what dreams and visions meant. It was always going to end this way.

Chapter 46

Joe

After binge-watching lots of TV and films, I've come to realise there are no such things as heroes or villains, just people making decisions. Take *Lex Luthor* in *Smallville.* If people were nicer to him whilst he was growing up, he would have never become *Superman's* nemesis. It was not his fault he's evil, it's everyone else's for treating him so badly at a young age. *Thanos* in *The Avengers*—he wouldn't feel the need to remove half the universe if the people of *Titan* didn't become so overpopulated and use all the planet's resources. He wouldn't think he would need to wipe out half the population of the universe if things had been different. So, other people's actions have caused him to think this way.

I never had a choice to kill those people. Dan's the one who wanted me arrested so he and Nikki can live a happy life together. DC and Sticks didn't have to steal from Leebee or force my hand by threatening to kill me. I didn't have to break that kid's arm if Sticks had wanted to kill him. None of this was my fault. It isn't what I wanted to do to get where I am… but it's done.

The first four days of staying in the new fancy house was a lot of fun. You get to eat when you want, sleep what you want and with no one to disturb you. Total freedom. After a while, you start to get bored. I grew tired of binge-watching films and *Netflix* series.

A couple of days ago some men dropped off a shit load of cocaine and money. There was so much money, I could have shoved it all in a swimming pool and done a backstroke on the pile of twenties and fifties. I needed some excitement while watching the next film. So I tried some of the cocaine. I lined it up a bit on the long cutting table, cut it up with a debit card. Rolled up a twenty and snorted. The inside of my nostrils burned, but I never got an instant rush, as they did in the films. So I'd try some more. Nope. I still feel the same. Maybe a third time.

Still nothing. That was disappointing. Best not have any more though, in case I overdose or take too much. Then I sat down to watch some shit film that was on. My heart began to race. I bounced on my seat.

Wow! Yeah!

I started to enjoy the film. Well, I think I enjoyed it. My body was racing that much I couldn't really concentrate on anything that was going off. God, I never felt so good. I wanted to go out and dance.

Later, I realised this could be a path to a slippery slope. I shouldn't do it all the time. I'd get addicted and owe Romeo lots and lots of money. The key is to have it in moderation. How hard could that be?

Chapter 47

Dan

The path I'd taken was as lonely as the road I walked on. Using the money I'd stolen from Gareth, I boarded the train to my Uncle Clive's quiet little town. The trek up narrow country roads were tough in the heat. The side of my face was burnt from the sun.

My mouth yearned for water, and my dark clothes were drenched in sweat. I gazed into the distance. The vast curved green country fields spread my sorrow into the open. Loneliness was not something I perceived until I met Nikki. How I miss her. How I wish she was here to enjoy this view with me, hand-in-hand. Without her, none of this scenery matters.

I made it to my uncle's stables. The horses slept under the sunset. The air was still warm, and I was in desperate need of a cool shower. Clouds began to assemble over the pointed rooftop. The wooden porch steps creaked as I made my way to the front door.

I turn to the right and notice the old rocking chair Uncle C used to sit on. It pointed towards, the one hole in the crest rail was an eye staring at me. The long wooden arms appeared as if they were reaching out to grab me. I ignored it.

I was too exhausted from the trekking and lack of sleep. I knocked on the door… no one answered. I tried again, with a little more gusto, then pressed my ear against the chipped door to listen for any movement. Silence.

I recalled my uncle having a spare key under a plant pot. I collected it, and let myself in.

I open the door to a drab and gloomy hallway. There was a vile smile smell in the air as if something had rotted away and been used to paint the walls. I turned my back to close the door. Once the door was shut, the smell had died. I stepped into the living room, which was not as dark and dingy as the corridor.

It was brightened by the silver chandelier on the ceiling, and the many candles spread around the room. My uncle sat on a single green tub chair. I sat tentatively opposite him, my bewildered eyes stared at his crumpled body. His grey hair was thickened and it ran over his shoulders.

This was not like him. He always tells me, "Long hair are for women only." His nails grew into pincers, and he looks twice as old as when I last saw him. His tired eyes see me, but he has no energy to speak. He's using all his power just to breathe. His breathing was aided by the nasal cannula, which was attached to a large oxygen tank beside him.

"You told me that you were going to die on your land."

That was the only thing I could say.

"I wanted to give it all to you."

He wheezed, then needed the time to recover from speaking a full sentence. While he was unable to yell at me, I decided to tell him everything that has happened and what I need to do next. Taking advantage of his vulnerability.

Time passed, I poured myself a cup of tea from the *Blue Willow* tea set. I took a sip. I wanted to spit it out… *It must have been the water again.* I placed the teacup back on the saucer, where it would remain.

Uncle Clive found the strength to talk again. "I understand you taking the car. But why do you need—"

He coughed. "Why do you need *that*?"

"I've really fucked this up, Granddad."

He inhaled as deep as his failing body would allow. "Told you not to call me that."

I dropped to my knees in front of him. I cried onto his lap. My tears stained his blue jeans.

"I tried, Uncle Clive. I really did try."

"Hey. Hey. It's okay."

He brushed my hair with his hands.

"I've ruined everything. I've lost Nikki and Joe. I tried to save them both. I really did. But I just fucked it up. I can't do anything right. I'm pathetic. I've always been pathetic. I'm just a sad miserable fuck-up, who can never do anything right."

The bawling worsened.

"And-and, I don't even deserve Nikki or Joe because I don't know if I really care about them—or anyone."

"You care about them enough to cry about it."

Sharp pain sliced through my body as if I were being cut open and all my insides poured out the floor.

"Rest, my boy. Take some rest. Tomorrow will be a new day," Uncle Clive advised.

"After tomorrow, I'll never be able to see you again."

"Even in death... we'll always love each other."

I regained my posture and slumped on the settee. The comforting words helped stitch my aching body, but not well enough—I still leaked from somewhere. My red eyes grew heavy, but the sound of a fly whizzing past me, caused me to gape at the little insect crawling on the rim of my teacup.

"Is something the matter?" my uncle asked.

"No, it's okay. It's just a fly in here."

I closed my eyes and rested my weary body.

I woke up the following morning on the settee. Uncle Clive was no longer sitting opposite me.

He might be out doing chores?

But he hasn't cleared last night's tea set. I spotted the cold undrunk tea on the side. The pot, saucers, spoons are all buried beneath dust. The silver chandelier was covered in cobwebs—the candlesticks had all been burnt out. Worst of all, that foul smell returned.

"Uncle Clive," I shouted while I walked up the creaky stairs. After I lifted my hand from the stair banister, it left a palm print on the surface. I wiped the filth from my hands onto my jeans.

When was the last time you cleaned this place?

As I approached the head of the stairs, the stench grew worse. A buzzing sound appeared from behind the door on the right. I pushed the door to his bedroom slowly.

"Uncle Clive," I called out.

There he was... lain on his rocking chair with his mouth open. Swinging back and forth. Flies swarmed around his decaying body.

Chapter 48

Joe

In my blue shorts, I bathe in the sun topping up my tan. I should be enjoying the sun, but I feel bored and miserable. It's the comedown after feeling so good from the night before. I feel the need for another pick-me-up. However, that is how people get addicted. I don't want to go down that route.

A short older woman across the road walks over in her high heels. Despite wearing high heels, this mature woman is still half my height. She is wearing skimpy denim shorts and a redshirt. Now she stands on the edge of my garden, with one short leg crossing over the other causing her to lean to one side. With one hand holding a picnic basket, her free hand plays with her long black curly hair.

"Good morning," she said, with a beam on her face.

"Morning."

I can feel my blood pumping now.

"I'm Caroline…"

Caroline is such a middle-class name.

"I live over the road. I just want to bring some of my homemade bread."

"Wow, thank you."

I stand up to take the basket from her. As I grab the basket from her, I feel her lustful green eyes ogle my brown six-pack.

"Are you living here on your own?" Carol asked.

"I do. My mum's away with her new boyfriend."

"Is it just you two?"

"It is. Thank you for the bread, Caroline. How can I repay you?"

She bites her bottom lip and gently sways her hips.

"There is something you can do for me…"

Am I in a porno, here?

"My fiancé is at work, and I need someone to carry a set of draws down to the skip. It's being collected today."

"I can do that for you, miss."

"Only if you don't mind."

"I'm free now."

Caroline's house is the exact same layout as mine. She leads me upstairs. My eyes fixate on her bum as it wiggles in and out of her revealing shorts. I use the screwdriver to dismantle the cream drawer cabinet. Carry the dismantled wood to the yellow skip outside, doing my best to scratch any of the fresh wall paint. I take the last piece of scrap to the garden. Walking back upstairs, Caroline waits for me on top of her beige bedding. I walk into the room, and she sits on the edge of the bed. The light from the window illuminates her pretty white smile and sinful green eyes.

"Would you like a drink?" she offered.

"Yes, please."

"How old are you?"

"Nineteen," I lied.

"So old enough for some wine?"

"I would love a glass."

"Wait here."

I remain on the edge of her soft fluffy bed covers, but my eyes snoop around the room. I spot something poking underneath the mirrored cupboard. It's similar to a few pieces of strings, but it's too thick to be part of cloth. I tip-toe to the object, gently pry into the cupboard. I giggle like a naughty schoolboy again. I'm shocked someone so nice, in a nice area, owns a black flogging whip.

"Like what you see?"

I leap ten spaces backwards. My heart pounds while I avoid eye contact with a grinning Caroline.

"I'm sorry, I didn't mean to. I thought I saw something. I thought it was a spider or some."

"It's okay. We're adults aren't we?"

Maybe, you are.

"There's no need to feel ashamed of our sexual urges. Me and my husband like to play games."

For the first time in a long time, a girl has made me speechless. I should get a grip. I'm a man now. I shouldn't be feeling intimidated. Maybe a glass of wine will settle my nerves. It does. I took a drink and it went straight to my head. I feel light and giddy.

"Do you like playing games? Mr—"

"It's—"

"Wait. Don't tell me your name. Let's keep it a mystery."

I place my glass down and walk over to her. Caroline stares into her glass of red wine. My body towers over her. She looks back up. returning her gaze back at me, eyes hungrier than before. I lean over to hold her warm back.

I feel it tensing with excitement. I move in to kiss her. Caroline's lower lip trembles, she knows she shouldn't do this—she shouldn't sleep with a younger man, especially when she's about to get married. Yet, she can't stop herself from submitting to her desire. We kiss, tasting the red wine from each other.

I brush my fingertips down the inside of her forearm, till I take the wine glass from her hand. As I walk over to put her glass beside mine, she takes her clothes off. I walk to Caroline, spin her around and reel her body in. Every inch of her soft back is pressed against my hard body. I put my hands around her neck and squeeze.

With my other hand, I massage her body from her small breast down to her hips. Caroline gasps as I kiss along the side of her neck until I reach the earlobe, then I begin to use my teeth. I sit on the foot of the bed. With tiny Caroline still in my grasp. My hand that's exploring her warm naked body is now being used to rub the most stimulating part of her body.

She wants to moan louder, but my grip around her throat is too tight. Caroline's hips can only stretch so far as my long hairy legs are wrapped around hers, restraining any movement.

Caroline can breathe again as the choking stops. She jumps back around, places both hands on my pectorals and kisses me gratefully. I stand up, holding Caroline by her black hair. Pull her on top of the foot of bed. Whilst she's on all fours, I make Caroline crawl to the head of the bed.

I form a claw with my hands to scratch down her smooth warm back till I reach her lower backside. There I slap one of her soft round cheeks, turning her white skin red.

I speak in a stern voice, "hold onto the rail and don't you dare let go."

"Yes."

She's forgotten to give me respect. I spank her again for punishment.

"Yes, *what?*"

"Yes, *sir.*"

"Good girl."

I spank her again as a reward.

I take my time walking over to the mirrored cabinet. I rummage through her selection of kinks in her closet of filth. Meanwhile, I occasionally glance back to see if Caroline has moved.

She remains on the bed, head down, holding on to the rail. Doing as she was told. I collect the handcuffs, gag, and the flogger. The click from the cuffs makes a satisfying sound to both of us.

When I was done, I could barely look at Caroline.

"You need to uncuff me because my fiancé will be home soon," Caroline pleaded.

I ignore her cry and put my shorts back on.

"Where are you doing? You need to untie me."

Walking out the house, I can still the bed rattling and the slave begging,

"Please. Please, come back. I don't want my boyfriend finding out."

I don't really know why I did it. Was it for the excitement of almost being caught? Is the need for respect and dominance really getting to me? Maybe, I just want to show her fiancé that you really can't trust anyone, not even those closest to you. Everyone betrays you or leaves you for someone else.

Chapter 49

Dan

I buried my uncle in his land, so he would dissolve into 'his earth'. I made a cross with two thick sticks and string. I'm not really a religious person. If there is a heaven, Uncle Clive would be up there in a younger form. Does that mean I will be going to hell? That's for God to judge. If there is such a thing. Why should I ask for his forgiveness? He was the one that left me in Desby, with no father figure and an alcoholic mother. Making a mockery of my own tormented soul for his own amusement.

Perhaps this life really is a test?

If so, I've failed. But, I imagined death was similar to sleep, without nightmares. Unaware of anything. No pain or suffering. Just peace.

Uncle Clive's face didn't look very peaceful.

No, it didn't. It looks like he died of a stroke or heart failure.
You knew he was ill, and you didn't do anything about it.
I know. After all, he had done for me, and I let him die alone. My fate will be the same, dead in the middle of nowhere with no one to find me for days—and it's what I deserve.

I lay low from Romeo and his crew by spending a few days on the farm. Mainly slept in the car. I didn't enter the house often, only to consume the last of the food. I couldn't stay here forever. The animals needed good care, and Romeo could track my whereabouts after he discovered Uncle Clive was my only other relative, apart from my mother.

A crow's caw had broken my concentration. I turned to see one hanging on the porch. Where the rocking chair was when I first arrived.

It was never really there, Dan. Like most horrible things—it was in your mind.

It flew over to sit on top of the scarecrow. A man with buttoned eyes, a straw hat, dickie bow, polka dot shirt and blue overalls—hung on a cross in the middle of the wheat field. He seemed to have collected more crows than usual. Four or five nested beside his head. At least he looked cheery about it—there was a bright smile drawn on top of the cloth.

I loaded the old banger with my uncle's long, dark raincoat, a duffle bag, and some antiques I pawned in the other village (not something I was proud of).

Another caw. I peered back, and the scarecrow had moved closer to the road.

You're seeing things again.

I went back into the house to get a flask of black coffee. Approaching the car, I noticed the scarecrow was now at the edge of the road. It still smiled at me, but the smile was longer and more unpleasant. It was more forced, wider, and sinister. For I knew the truth—it was never really happy.

A crow landed on top of the car, it's dark eyes wanted to swallow me up. It cawed, but the sound from its beak wasn't a typical caw, it was shrieking a name.

"Joe. Joe."
Joe's in trouble!

I left the farm, taking my granddad's car, and his shotgun with me.

Part 5 – Monsters

Chapter 50

Vascular surgeon Dr Richard Vaughn sat in his darkroom alone. Supping on the single malt whisky. The luxurious taste sends a burning sensation down his throat. In a drunken stupor, he eyes the tumbler whilst stirring it with the palm of his hands. The steady hands are not so calm tonight.

Richard saved this drink for a special occasion… his wedding night. He's not so sure the wedding will go ahead anymore. After spending all day saving someone's life, by diverting the blood around a woman's abdominal aortic aneurysm via a graft he had come home to this. It had been a difficult case.

All he wanted to do was go home and have an early night. When arriving home, he found his fiancé naked and handcuffed to the bed. She was having an affair with a younger man. The kid across the street. Dr Vaughn's stomach wrenches at the idea of his hands all over his soon-to-be wife. He can't look at her anymore. Resentment causes an invisible glass pane that now stands between them.

Why such a young boy? It is borderline paedophilia.

Richard grew envious. He's not the young man he once was at medical school. His hair was grey, the beer belly was harder to trim and due to the nature of his work he wasn't home much.

I understand Caroline needs some affection, but I've just been so busy. When I drive all the way back from work, I'm exhausted.

Still, his grasp around the glass tumbler tightens. The more he thinks about this younger lothario having his way with Caroline, the more he wants to march over the road and beat him to a pulp.

Richard leans back on his leather armchair sipping more of the liquid nourishment for enticing the rage.

How can I tell people? How can I tell my friends my stag do is off? Ronnie and James, those two crazy buffoons, were really looking forward to it. God knows what they were planning. Knowing them, it'll be something excessive. Now I have to look at them in the eyes and tell them the truth. I'll always be known as the guy whose fiancé cheated on him, a week before they were meant to get married. I'll have everyone's pitiful eyes dawning on me constantly. Feeling sorry for poor old Richard Vaughn.

Richard's thoughts start to take a dark turn.

I could kill the boy… he's ruined my life… I'll take his… However, I could lose my license to practice… unless someone does it for me.

The surgeon recalled saving a woman's life. Henrietta was her name. She had a son, who was ever so thankful. A mean-looking chap. Neck tattoos. A well-disciplined military man. Always wearing a freshly ironed suit. He wears shades often, but when the glasses were off, I saw those eyes. Eyes that had seen true horror. War. Though, I believe he mentioned he's not in the armed forces anymore.

He now works as a personal security guard for a high-profile investor. It all sounds shady to Dr Vaughn. The man did say, "If there's anything, *anything*." All I need to do is ring the number on his card.

Richard isn't sure why he ever kept it. Dr Vaughn took pride in saving lives, he also believes this other man is the opposite.

I'm not sure if I can live with myself. But it's definitely worth something to consider…

Chapter 51

Dan left his uncle's crumbling motor in the street behind Desby Hospital. He walked into the hospital ward and searched for the nearest available nurse. Most people were on the ward rounds. There were so many patients and so few members of staff. However, one nurse was free.

"Excuse me, I'm doing a presentation on personal protective equipment at school. I was wondering if I could please take some home for the demonstration?"

Despite being rushed off her feet, the nurse still presented a pleasant smile.

"Of course, just don't tell anyone you got it from me."

"I won't. Thank you."

The bonny blonde brought Dan shoe covers, an eye visor, an apron, a face mask and disposable gloves. He recreated the image of the nurse he saw outside the maternity ward when he went to see Nikki and Alfie. Dan realised the only thing missing was the hairnet. His escapade took him back to the maternity ward. Along the way, Dan questioned how he was going to break into the theatre and steal a hairnet.

Luckily, a porter from the store's department brought a delivery of items. In the midst of different boxes, was a delivery of blue hats. Dan watched as the overweight delivery boy left the shipment unattended. At that moment, Dan took his chance, opened the rusty cage on wheels and pinched a singular blue hairnet.

Dan returned to the car. Inside he tried on the face mask. After looping the string around his ears, he pinched the metal bar across his nose. He felt like *Bane* in *The Dark Knight Rises.* Dan impersonated the *Batman* villain's breathing, then tried to imitate his voice, "*I am Gotham's reckoning… I am necessarily evil.*" He chuckled to himself. It would have been funny if Joe was here…

But he's not here.

Dan had no time to waste—there was something he needed to do. Perhaps wearing a mask is essential to not only hide your identity but for the encouragement to be someone bigger and stronger.

Chapter 52

It wasn't until 8:00 p.m. when the rain began to pour. Thunder roared in the sky, but it was okay—Leebee wasn't going anywhere. It was his shift to sit in the red *Toyota* and spy on Nikki Yakes. He bit into his sandwich, not really hungry, just bored.

Leebee hated this detail. He normally passes it off to one of the other guys. However, it's his turn tonight. He'd sit in this car till the sun shone. Making sure Nikki doesn't take Alfie somewhere she shouldn't. Somewhere that's anywhere out of Desby. The rain fell thick and fast. The water made the car's windows less visible. The droplets danced around the pane causing the house to look blurry.

Leebee browsed rear-view mirror. He noticed a long dark figure walking towards him.

"Who's *dis* madhead?"

As the figure draws near to the car, Leebee can see the rainwater flowing through the ripples of the extra-long raincoat. He tried to recognise the face, but it was shadowed by the hood. The mysterious form was almost by the car, Leebee could hear the boots splashing on the puddles below. Leebee spied out of the side mirror, he could see something long and round from his right arm sleeve.

Is it a crutch?

Leebee was unsettled when the figure in the long raincoat stood an inch away from his door. Rainwater drops off the hood as he looks down to scrutinise the driver.

"Get out of here," Leebee warned.

It does not move.

"Step off, bro. You don't know who you're messing *we*."

The mixture of heavy rain and the window barrier causes Leebee's threats to sound muffled.

"Dude, you hear me?"

Leebee rolled the window down.

"I said—"

Leebee was suddenly silenced. As the double-barrel end of a shotgun is pressed against his cheek.

Leebee raises his hands in the air, "Wow-wow-wow-wow. Take it easy, man. *Wha' ya* want. I'd *ge* it to you. I swear."

A rough gritty tone voice appeared from underneath the hood.

"Where's Joe Smith?"

"I can *ge ya* the address."

"You're going to take me to him."

"Okay-okay. Please don't shoot."

Leebee unlocks the car. The figure in the raincoat sat behind the gangster. With one hand, the mysterious person dug the shotgun into the back of the driver's seat. With his free hand, Dan removes the hood from his raincoat.

Leebee recognised him. He was wearing one of those hospital masks, but it wasn't much of a disguise.

You're Daniel, who dated Nikki.

Although, he didn't want to say anything, in case it gave Dan a reason to shoot him in the back. Leebee could feel the shotgun digging from the seat.

"Give me your phone," Dan ordered.

"Bruv, *ya* don't wanna do *dis.* Trust me."

"I said give me your phone!" Leebee unwillingly imparted the phone to his captor. Dan took his mobile, rolled out of the window, and threw it out.

"*Dat* shit's brand new man. You owe me for *dat.*"

"Shut up and drive. One more word from you and I'll shoot you and leave you to bleed out slowly."

Leebee started the engine.

***

In the dead of night, a plain white van is parked by the red cobblestone path. The two people inside gaze past the fake plastic tree, to study the newly built modern home. They were aware, the kitchen had a long conservatory-esque door;

however, they'll be a camera shining over the enormous garden. The best way to get access is through the front door. Modern uPVC doors are easily breakable. They don't need to break it, they have a key.

"Where did you get that?" one guy asked.

"He gave it to me," the other replied while putting on his balaclava.

***

Leebee drove down the motorway cautiously. Lights from the other vehicles were intertwining blurred shapes. The torrential weather caused the roads to be less visible. The gun, poking from behind, was hurting his back.

Dan was unsettled about how normal this felt. He assumed there would be an urge to vomit again, a rise in temperature, or shaking at least. The numbness had returned. That's what frightened him the most. *This* should not have felt normal. He compared himself to his hostage. Leebee was cool, he didn't sweat, or shake. His eyes seemed to be unfazed by the events.

This is what you're turning into Dan… a monster.

***

Joe was unable to fall asleep that night. He couldn't remember the last time he had more than four hours at night. He thought it would change. He'd believed he would get a good night's rest if he moved out into a safer house on a safe street.

Out of boredom, he thought it might be a good idea to count how much money he's been asked to store within the walls of the house. A bit like counting sheep, he hoped this would make him nod off. The bag was heavy, it's close to dead lifting a collection of concrete blocks. He placed wrapped banknotes onto the table beside his single cream settee.

***

The two guys in balaclavas creep along the fake grass and use the key to enter the new modern home.

Leebee parks outside Joe's new home.

"Is this it?" Dan asked while simultaneously prodding the shotgun further into Leebee.

"Yeah. You gonna let me go?"

"Not yet. Get out the car."

Leebee followed his instructions. He got out of the *Toyota*, hands still raised in the air. Dan was a second behind. He kept the shotgun in the direction of Leebee's chest. In the heat of the moment, Leebee didn't realise it had stopped raining.

Dan unzipped his long black raincoat, it dropped to the floor. This revealed a white plastic apron and a large bum bag that Dan had been carrying around his shoulders.

"Walk inside the house."

"You want me to go in?"

"Fucking move."

Leebee reluctantly followed his commands.

"Open the door," Dan commanded while he was taking off his boots on the porch. Leebee noticed Dan was wearing latex gloves, whereas he wasn't. Leebee realised it'll be his fingerprints around the house.

Am I being set up?

***

Joe had finished offloading the bag of money onto the table. Just as he was about to sit down, he heard someone close the front door to his house.

***

The two guys entered the living room, they crept on the polished floor tiles.

"Not here," one man whispered.

They manoeuvre stealthily around the stainless kitchen worktops and oak cabinets in the kitchen. They sneak into the main bedroom and find their target sleeping under the covers.

It was almost as if they had communicated telepathically. The two marauders simultaneously prepared to pounce on their prey. They were expecting him to be asleep, but he had the upper hand. The person leapt out of bed. The bed sheets flew in the intruder's direction, this caused the two guys to flinch.

"What are you doing in my house?" Dr Richard Vaughn asked.

"We're here to kidnap you for your stag do," James yelled.

Ronnie took off his balaclava, "We're going to Ibiza, baby."

"I knew you guys would do something completely imprudent," the surgeon laughed.

All three guys huddled, arms locked around each other's shoulders, and jumped up and down like they were school kids again.

***

Joe was gobsmacked. Leebee had just plodded into his living room, followed by Dan wearing gloves, aprons, shoe covers over his socks, a hairnet, eye protection, and wielding a shotgun.

Chapter 53

Dan used the handle of the shotgun to knock out Leebee. His body tumbled onto the floor, blood poured out of the wound and stained the furry rug.

"What are you doing here, Dan?" Joe questioned.

Dan noticed that Joe didn't appear to be agitated by having a shotgun pointed at him.

"Put your hands up."

Dan wanted to sound stern, but it came out as a mere whisper.

Joe ignored Dan. "We both know, you're not gonna shoot me."

"I said put your hands up."

Dan repeated, he spoke through his teeth.

"No, Dan. I'm not."

Joe sat down on his cream settee, next to the table of money. He noticed Dan's body was jittery and his wild eyes kept switching between him and the money.

"Money. Is that what you want? Money? You can take it."

"I don't want money."

Joe and Dan stared long and hard into each other's eyes. Trying to see what's in their minds or what remained of their souls. A silent pause caused seconds to turn to minutes. Time passed slowly.

Dan broke the silence, "I wanted to save you, and Nikki. I tried to kill Romeo. But, I failed."

"I don't need saving, Dan."

"Yes, you do. That's why I am here."

"Who do I need saving from?"

"Yourself, Joe. I'm here to preserve you. *You,* for who you really are. My charming, arrogant, handsome, blue-eyed friend. Before you turn into another monster."

"Do you realise how insane you sound? I'm not surprised how crazy you are. With your abusive alcoholic mum, your depressing books, the sad music, your dad leaving, and all the times the other kids kicked the shit out of you."

"Your mom's a saint. Why did you turn so easily?"

"My mum left me, just like you did. I had to be a man. I had to be strong to survive."

"I guess we're both products of our environment."

"We were always better than everyone, Dan. We both had a bright future outside of Desby."

"We were supposed to leave together," said Dan, with tears dripping from his eyes.

"That was your fault, not mine."

Dan inhaled deeply and raised his shoulders.

Joe surrendered. "I'm not mad anymore. Look at this nice house. In this nice estate. All I wanted to do was to feel *safe,* and now I am."

"Safe!" Dan spat. "Pick up that money beside you."

"Dan."

"Do it! Pick some of that money up and hold it in your arms," Dan yelled.

Joe leant to his left, grabbing handfuls of wrapped twenty-pound notes. Meanwhile, he kept a watchful eye on Dan and his shaking hands. Joe sat up straight, squeezed the bundle of wrapped cash against his body as if it were armour.

Dan's eyes moved from the shotgun to the heap of twenty-pound notes, which shielded Joe's body.

"Do you feel *safe now*?"

Joe went to stand up. "Dan—"

Dan fired the shotgun, causing burnt and torn banknotes to fling up into the air. They scattered and fluttered onto the ground and rested beside the rocking settee.

Chapter 54

Nikki was at home, exhausted. It took forever to get Alfie to settle. Awake in the middle of the night, crying for food. She would have had some vodka to help her get back to sleep, if that arsehole, Dan hadn't gotten into her head. She played with her hair in the mirror, wondering, which colour to dye it next. The doorbell rang repeatedly, waking up the once restful baby. The baby's cry echoed throughout the house.

'*Grrrrr*'. Nikki's temper reached boiling point. She slammed her feet down each step of the staircase, as screams at the door,

"Don't you realise what fucking time it is? I've just got Alfie to settle you bastards. You're gonna have to come in here and cradle him back to sleep. Mark my words. I'll make you fucking do it."

She hurled open the front door, ready to yell at the person behind it, but there was no one there.

Nikki looked down to see a large duffle bag.

What is this?

She studied the outside of the sack cautiously. Then leant over to slowly undo the zip. Hoping nothing pops out to scare her. Her eyes sparkled when she saw the contents. Money. Lots and lots of wrapped up twenties.

Alfie was still bawling relentlessly, but Nikki couldn't leave this much on the ground. A car drove past the house. It was a right dump. It was so old; it might as well have been held together by duct tape. There was a note in the side pocket.

Live your best life in Australia. I'm sorry. Love, Dan.

She went out in her bare feet, to chase the car. By the time she got down the steps of her house, he had gone. So had the red *Toyota*. The time was now. With no one watching, she could leave Desby. Nikki piled lots of clothes on top of the cash. Settled Alfie in a shoulder strap.

I don't know what you've done, Dan. There's enough in here for two passports and flights to Australia.

A peculiar mixture of fear and excitement caused Nikki's heart to beat fast. It all happened so fast she didn't know what to do.

I'll call for a taxi, give a fake name. Drive up north to a hotel. Ring for a second taxi, give another fake name and drive somewhere else. I'll ask mum to forward me the passports when they arrive.

Nikki eventually came to her senses. She couldn't disappear now. It would seem suspicious. Victor would know that she had the money and not Dan. She had to wait, wait for the passports to arrive and then take another opportunity to escape to the airport. She unstrapped Alfie from the baby harness and let him sleep in his cot for another night.

I just hope you've caused a big enough distraction long enough for my passport to arrive.

Chapter 55

A few hours before Nikki received the money, Dan filled the duffle bag with the remainder of the cash from the table. It must have been thousands of pounds. Dan avoided looking at Joe. He couldn't bring himself to see what he had done, or his best friend with a massive hole in his chest.

Leebee was still unconscious. Dan pulled out the rope from his large bum bag and tied him to a chair. He's had plenty of experience lifting a body from when his mum had passed out drunk. Dan scanned the house for something he could use against Romeo. He found the jackpot, cocaine! Lots and lots of cocaine. He filled another duffle bag with the stuff.

Dan filled the car with the bags containing money and drugs,

This could go badly wrong if I get stopped by the police.

He went back inside to check on Leebee and Joe. Leebee had woken up and must have attempted to break free because he lay on his side. His forehead hit the tiled floor. He looks at Dan with such spiteful eyes. It was probably a good thing Dan couldn't hear what Leebee was trying to scream from underneath the duct tape gag.

Dan took one last view of Joe. Dan never saw the seventeen-year-old with a bullet wound in the middle of his body. No. He saw a muscular ten-year-old boy with blonde hair and brown skin, resting his tired blue eyes. Forever young and free. No longer troubled with the adult world.

The sound of the ocean waves flew in and out of Dan's ears. Then he heard the sound of his and his friends' younger selves—laughing and joking. He smelt the salty sea air. Felt the sand on his feet, and an arm around his shoulder... *we'll always be best friends.*

That vision died within an instant. Dan was left standing in a dark room, looking down at the mess he made. He wanted to cradle Joe in his arms, to cry alongside him. Put his hands through his hair and feel his touch one last time. Dan knew he couldn't, it would have defeated the whole purpose of the PPE because it would leave some kind of trace.

Dan couldn't take any more of Leebee's muffled pleads. He kneeled down over his captive's slanted head and ripped the duct tape from over his mouth. Leebee cringed as the tape was torn off from his skin then breathed deeply from his mouth before asking,

"Are you going to kill me?"

Dan took his time to answer, "No, I'm going to do something worse…"

Leebee looked terrified.

"I'm going to let you live."

Leebee's short, terrified period morphed into a state of confusion.

Dan stood back up.

"No matter where you go, we'll find you," Leebee warned.

"I have a feeling you won't. Because *I* don't even know where I am going."

Dan's vague response only bewildered the gangster even further. Leebee tried hard to wriggle his way free, but the rope was too tight—and he couldn't get up from the floor. He could scream for help, but he would have to explain how he got here and who the dead person is.

Dan parked the red *Toyota* full of drugs, on the premises of Victor Romeo's restaurant—*Giovanni's*. When Dan anonymously called the police the following morning, it was enough for them to issue a warrant. Romeo was never convicted. Life isn't what it appears to be on TV—but it was enough to keep him distracted for a while. Especially, after a detective found a note book containing the times and places of some of the drug trafficking.

After Dan walked over to Nikki's to collect his uncle's car, he dropped off the bag full of money at Nikki's,

She's going to be so pissed at me, for waking her and Alfie up at 3:00 a.m.

Dan saw Nikki for the last time. It was not the romantic parting he wanted it to be. It was a mere glimpse through the rear-view mirror. He drove to the YOU ARE NOW LEAVING DESBY sign. Underneath it, Dan came to a halt and killed the engine. He sat in silence, took slow deep breaths, and fixed his eyes on the open road in front of him. His hands twisted around the steering wheel. Dan's face turned red as he burst into tears. His skinny body shook, his teeth clenched and then he head-butted the centre of the steering wheel. Over and over again, until there was a cut on his forehead. When his head couldn't take anymore, Dan punched the dashboard until his knuckles bled. Dan knew this day would arrive. He was almost liberated; however, loneliness was his passenger. Sure, he had some money in his pocket, survival skills passed on from Uncle Clive, and enough knowledge to gain employment. There was still a yearning for companionship.

I suppose. without someone else… I could be whoever I wanted to be.

Dan recalled what he said before meeting Nikki.

I liked "the idea of being on the road, being hunted down, never to be found. Living in a tent in the north of Scotland sounds appealing. Waking up to a sunrise, with the light reflecting on top of the calm, blue waters of Loch Lomond. I could wild camp anywhere. Not necessarily Scotland. I could be anywhere and be anything. Be someone else, someone who's better than me. Impersonate a more charming, and confident character. Instead of being a shy skinny loser, with fluffy hair."

Dan started the car. He felt himself changing as the car trailed out of Desby. Like a snake shedding its skin, he was leaving an old part of him behind. Remoulded. Born again.

He recalled what Nikki once told him, "*So, whenever I'm not here. Or when you leave town to pursue your dreams. This is something to help remember me by. You will listen to this song, and a part of me will be with you for those three minutes.*"

The radio in the car did not work, but when Dan drove—he heard the song *All I Have Left is You* as clear as any speaker. A drum began to beat softly. The subdued piano followed. A soft vocalist delicately sang about how complicated relationships are. Then a guitarist swayed a few notes melodically. The explosive chorus kicked in… Dan's mind was blown away.